CÚCHULAINN
~ AND THE ~
# CROW QUEEN

Cúchulainn
∽ and the ∽
Crow Queen

BERNARD KELLY

ILLUSTRATIONS AND ADDITIONAL MATERIAL BY JUNE PETERS

In memory of
Gary Henry and Rob Peters

First published 2014

The History Press Ireland
50 City Quay
Dublin 2
Ireland
www.thehistorypress.ie

British Library Cataloguing in Publication Data.
A catalogue record for this book is available from the British Library.

ISBN 978 1 84588 816 9

Typesetting and origination by The History Press

ANCIENT LEGENDS RETOLD:
AN INTRODUCTION TO THE SERIES

This book represents a new and exciting collaboration between publishers and storytellers. It is part of a series in which each book contains an ancient legend, reworked for the page by a storyteller who has lived with and told the story for a long time.

Storytelling is the art of sharing spoken versions of traditional tales. Today's storytellers are the carriers of a rich oral culture, which is flourishing across Britain and Ireland in storytelling clubs, theatres, cafés, bars and meeting places, both indoors and out. These storytellers, members of the storytelling revival, draw on books of traditional tales for much of their repertoire.

The partnership between The History Press and professional storytellers is introducing a new and important dimension to the storytelling revival. Some of the best contemporary storytellers are creating definitive versions of the tales they love for this series. In this way, stories first found on the page, but shaped 'on the wind' of a storyteller's breath, are once more appearing in written form, imbued with new life and energy.

My thanks go first to Nicola Guy, a commissioning editor at The History Press, who has championed the series, and secondly to my friends and fellow storytellers, who have dared to be part of something new.

Fiona Collins, Series Originator, 2014

Introduction

When Patrick came to Ireland, the High King refused to accept his new religion until the saint had raised Cúchulainn from the dead.

Exhumed, the great Ulster hero recounted his victories:

> 'I played on breaths
> Above the horses steam
> Before me on every side
> Great battles were broken.'

Cúchulainn then urged the king to turn away from his old gods and embrace this new sky god and escape the fate he himself now endured, an eternity in hell.

In this story, grafted onto the end of the Ulster Cycle, Cúchulainn acts as the bridge between the old ways and the new. It captures a mythic moment in time when a fluid oral pagan tradition was being transformed into a Christianised one, forever fixed to the page. With this tangible object came unfamiliar ideas of ownership and novel notions of possession. From this point on, these stories no longer needed to live in our beings or in the naming of the land to survive, but could be carried around outside ourselves.

The second patron saint of Ireland, Columcille, once visited Finnian, the Abbot of Moille. Taking a book from his host's library, he secretly copied it out. When the king proclaimed,

'To every cow her calf. To every book its copy', laying down the first laws of copyright, Columcille refused to be bound by the judgment and give his copy back. In 561, he and his clan faced the king's forces and although he won this battle of the book, when he saw the bodies of the slaughtered, he realised what he had done and sailed away from Ireland.

This left only one Irish patron saint still in situ – Brigid, who, as well as giving her name to Britain, was a recycled version of the Celtic goddess of storytelling. The Morrigu, the great Crow Queen, a battle goddess akin to Freya in the Norse tradition, who dealt in sex, death and cows, was not to be so easily incorporated into the new pantheon of saints. Although she struck a very different sense of awe to the one being propagated by the monks of the time, they still managed to preserve her in some of her glory in the texts they transcribed.

It was the power of words that brought Columcille back to Ireland in 590 on a mission to stop the poets and storytellers being expelled from the land. The king had become tired of the savagery of their satires, which sometimes caused even fierce warriors to drop dead from shame. Columcille argued that it was their praise songs and their stories that would keep the king's memory alive long after he was dead:

> 'If poets verses be but fables
> So be food and garments fables
> So is the entire world a fable
> So is man of dust a fable.'

The storytellers stayed, but under stricter control. The warrior women of Ireland were not so fortunate. They were banned and the possibility of having a warrior queen like Medb, a visible representation of feminine sovereignty, was extinguished.

Cúchulainn was resurrected once again at the end of the nineteenth century, when writers such as Standish O'Grady refashioned dusty academic texts into a popular myth of national identity equivalent to the corpus of Arthurian legend. When this

Celtic revival was in full flow, Cúchulainn's hyper-masculinity was appealing to a literary elite, who, while extolling the earthy virtues of the peasant poor, rarely got their hands dirty themselves. He was seen as an embodiment of self-determination, a great defender of an embattled people. Some tried to turn the Celtic Titan into a clean-cut Achilles, while others revelled in him being an out-of-control killing machine whose rage destroyed everything in his way.

'We may one day have to devote ourselves to our own destruction so that Ireland can be free,' wrote Pádraig Pearse, believing that 'bloodshed is a cleansing and sanctifying thing and a nation which regards it as the final horror has lost its manhood'.

Pearse was born in 1879, when O'Grady's version of Cúchulainn was first published in his *History of Ireland*. As he grew, Pearse became imbued with the passion of this hero's life, seeing it as symbolising 'the redemption of man by a sinless god ... like a retelling (or is it a foretelling?) of the story of Calvary'. Aged 19, he had already published a series of lectures on Cúchulainn, and ten years later he opened St Enda's, a bilingual school aimed at countering the oppressive forces of the English education system, which he dubbed 'the murder machine'.

The front hall of St Enda's was dominated by a fresco of Cúchulainn taking arms and the words 'I care not though I live but one day and one night, if only my name and deeds live after me'. The students used a Cúchulainn primer for the Irish language and each assembly brought a story from the Ulster Cycle.

They joked that Cúchulainn was virtually a member of staff, but the school curriculum was no laughing matter. A boy at St Enda's was as likely to be given a rifle as a Bible on prize-giving day and evenings were spent making hand grenades under the supervision of the science master.

On Easter Monday 1916, Pearse and his comrades, including thirty of the boys, stormed the General Post Office building in Dublin. On its steps, Pearse read a proclamation declaring Ireland free. His command of poetical rhetoric mesmerized many of those who heard him. Newsboys distributed a printed version throughout the city.

When Pearse stepped out of the burning building, he emerged into the inferno of his own myth. He became a symbol of national desire, both Celtic hero and Catholic martyr when he was executed four days later.

In 1935, the most famous image of Cúchulainn, a pagan pieta, was unveiled in the GPO building in Dublin; a final fusing of Pearse's memory into the story of the Ulster champion he adored. This representation, like most depictions of Cúchulainn's death, features his nemesis, the Crow Queen, perched on his shoulder. She is the mistress of chaos; he is her creature and it is his refusal of her advances that brings him down in the end.

By the end of the twentieth century, Cúchulainn was resurrected yet again, cloaked in a Union flag and claimed in public murals as an 'ancient defender of Ulster from Irish attacks over two thousand years'. This appropriation of the myth never really took hold. He was being set up to defend borders and fight foes that for him never existed. It is said that stories are like hungry ghosts. If left untold, they demand to be lived. Cúchulainn, it seems, will continue to be brought back to life as long as the red-mouthed Goddess holds sway in our world.

1

Disputes

Three sisters, three one-eyed midwives, met at the crossroads. Above them there turned the constellations of the sky. At their feet skulked a hungry whelp of a hound.

~

'How did it all begin?' asked the youngest sister.

'With the battle,' said the oldest one. 'When the gods came from the north, they set their ships alight so there could be no turning back. Their dark goddess, the Morrigu, the great Crow Queen, descended and pierced the earth with her sharp claws. She stood astride the river of tomorrow's battle and what was to come began to bubble up from out of its depths; heads, fingers, eyes and teeth. Picking through the bits and pieces, she began to stitch all together again; limb back to limb, hand back to arm, scalp back to head. With sinew and song, seamlessly she did her work, washing away the blood from the dead-eyed boys not yet born, cleaning their corpses, bathing their bodies, breaking their bones.

'Then came himself, the Dagda, Old Fat Belly, a god with appetites equal to hers. Dragging that mighty thing that hung between his legs, ploughing it into the earth, he separated the land from the sea and the sea from the sky. With a stomach the circumference of a world, copulation would be tricky, but she, the seasoned war goddess, was used to difficult manoeuvres.

He caressed the nine untied tresses of her hair and with each move towards her, the bodies floating on the current between them shuddered and gasped; lungs spluttered out fluid and filled with air.

'Shaking and shivering, hollow-eyed men emerged out of the dark waters and were dried by the beat of her wings as she took to the air. Their fists grabbed spears as above them she soared. Yelling, they ran towards her other children on the other side. Eye to eye, hand to hand, they hacked at each other, spears humming overhead; the clashing of shields, the clatter of swords, the slicing through flesh, the piercing of points passing through skin, the strokes and the blows of the weapons. Side by side, pride fought with shame that day and both stumbled on ground slippery with blood.

'Through the killing, the craftsmen made good, sharpening blades blunted by bone; refixing spearheads embedded in flesh. The carpenters stripped the felled trees, worked the wood and turned the forests into smooth shafts of light. The masters of metal mended what was broken, their bellows blowing sparks that flew as stars into the sky. The braziers melded and riveted all together again.

'Above, the Crow Queen surveyed the slaughter, saw the fires die down and watched as two great beings met on the plain.

'One had a great eye, a black hole, the eyelid pierced by rings of gold, pulled open by chains of iron. A look and you shrivel and die.

'The other was a dancing deity, tracing the patterns of the sun across the face of the earth. He held a sharpened ray of light.

'"Who stands before me now?" asked Balor, the one-eyed god.

'"The one you tried to keep in the dark," answered Lugh, the shining lad.

'"I live in the dark," said Balor, "Are you kin of mine?"

'"I am the son of the daughter you kept locked in a tower without windows or words so that I would not be born into this world."

'"Yet you stand before me now," said the unseeing one.

'"You shut out the light, but the sun kept on rising."

'"Then, blood of mine, let me look at you."

'His warriors pulled on the chains and the eye began to open. Balor only saw the point of light just before it hit and burned.

'Lugh stepped forward, turned his spear in the socket and took out the still staring eye. He held it high, a ball of light now ablaze in the sky.

'Rising out of the guts of the dead, she, the Crow Queen, laughed.

'"Even a god cannot outwit his own fate."

'Ascending into the air, she crowed over the battle won and sang the end of the world.

> 'I see a cursed land:
> summers without bloom,
> orchards without fruit,
> cattle without milk,
> oceans without life.

> 'There will be kings without courage,
> old men without wisdom,
> judges without justice,
> women without sovereignty.

> 'Every son will enter his mother's bed,
> every father will enter his daughter's bed,
> each brother will become his own brother's brother-in-law,
> each sister will become her own sister's mother.

> 'The whole earth
> consumed by fire,
> as my shadow
> devours the sun.'

'Sister, you end everything too soon,' said the youngest one-eyed one.

Snow began to fall and the three midwives built a fire. The hound rested his head on each lap in turn, as three eyes stared into the flames.

⌇

'How did it all begin?' asked the middle sister.

'With the bulls,' said the youngest one. 'Of all the gifts the new gods brought; the shining spear of the sun; the everlasting cauldron of plenty; the screaming stone of destiny; surely the greatest one was the pig.

'The gods had two pig keepers called Bristle and Grunt and although their masters, the god of the North and the god of the South, were fierce rivals, their swineherds were firm friends. "You know where you are with a pig," said Bristle.

'"Yes," said Grunt, gazing into the eyes of his favourite sow. "They are the most faithful of creatures."

'"Not like a sheep," said Bristle.

'"Certainly not like a sheep," said Grunt. "You would not confide in a sheep."

'"You would not," said Bristle. "Foolish animals, sheep."

'"Thick as pig shit," said Grunt.

'"And what is this obsession with bulls?" asked Bristle. "Sure they have the balls, but do they have the brains of a pig?"

'"No they do not", said Grunt. "They are too belligerent."

'"Yes. Pigs," sighed Bristle. "You could tell anything to a pig and know that the confidence would be kept."

'"Indeed it would," said Grunt, "for a pig shapes a man into being a better human being."

'"Aye," said Bristle. "A pig is a friend you can eat."

'"And there's no finer thing in the world than that," said Grunt.

'The two pig keepers were well matched. If acorns rained down in the south, Grunt would invite Bristle and his pigs to the feast. If they rained down in Bristle's territory then Grunt and his pigs would head north. So it was year after year, the pigs getting fatter and fatter and then fed to the gods to give them that everlasting life they so enjoyed.

'But the gods have a habit of intruding even into the peaceful world of pigs. The gods of the North and South each wanted their herd to be the biggest and the best. They put pressure on their pig keepers to outdo each other or else they might find themselves out of a job. At first, nothing changed, but soon they began to talk and meet a bit less. Then one day when the acorns rained down in the south, Bristle was not invited to come. Grunt was never asked to come north again after that. And he cast a spell over Bristle's pigs so no matter how much they ate they would not grow fat. Then Bristle cast the same spell over Grunt's pigs and both were sacked for having skinny swine.

'Deprived of their beloved companions, the ex-pig keepers became bitter and started to bicker and quarrel.

'"I always had the biggest pigs," said Bristle.

'"Mine always had the tastiest flesh," said Grunt.

'And so it went on until, one day, their own bile became so unbearable that they turned into two birds of prey. Taking to the air as Talon and Claw, they cried of the beauty of pigs and the foolishness of kings.

'Then diving down into the waters, they turned into two fishes – Ebb and Flow, spending days devouring each other in the depths.

'Out onto the land they became two stags – Push and Shove, rutting in the spring.

'Then two warriors – Point and Edge, endlessly slaying each other across the plain.

'Then two banshees – Boundary and Space, wailing at the windows of the dying.

'Then they fell to earth as two maggots, wriggling on the ground where they were eaten up by two cows, out of which they burst as two young bulls who within one day grew into the most magnificent creatures the land had ever seen: the great brown bull of Ulster, the Donn Cuailage, and the mighty white bull of Connacht, the Finnbennach. A hundred warriors could stand in their shadows; fifty youths could play games across their backs. Each bulled fifty heifers every day, the calves born out of their mothers the next.'

The three sisters sharpened three stakes of rowan, pressed point against skin and three drops of blood fell on the frozen ground. The hungry hound lapped it all up.

'How did it all begin?' asked the oldest midwife.

'With the birth pangs,' said the youngest one. 'When men lost their sense of wonder and stopped evoking the old gods, those who had once been worshipped retreated into the hills and the hedgerows.

'There was a farmer whose wife had died. He knew about crops and cattle, but to care for the four boys she had left behind, now, that was a different kind of task. The farmer was handsome and women liked him well enough, but none were eager to enter a dead woman's bed so soon.

'Then, one day, a quiet woman slipped into the house. He could not remember her knocking or saying good day. Just one day there she was, sitting by the hearth staring into the fire. Nothing was said. He nodded. She nodded back as if this had always been their custom. She put the bread on the table and no questions were asked about who she was or where she was from. He was not a curious man. And anyhow there was work to be done and children to be fed, and he knew never to look a gift horse in the mouth. Now on the farm, everything was done quicker and better than before. The cow's milk tasted creamier and the farmer grew richer. Then one night as easily as she had come into the house, the farmer found she had slipped into bed beside him. Lovemaking was as quiet as everything else she did and as finely judged.

'He awoke to find her place in the bed empty and cold. He called for her. She did not come. He wrapped the blankets around himself and opened the door to the outside world. There on the hill, under the stars, he saw her. Yoked to the plough, she was turning the earth as easily as a woman turns her head. Then she saw him and slipping out of the harness and moving with the swiftness of a steed, she stood before him and spoke. "Promise to tell no one what you have seen. Promise."

'He promised.

'One day, word came from the king; an invitation to the yearly horse fair.

'"Don't go," she pleaded. "My time is near. The new ones will soon be coming."

'"I won't be gone for long," he said. "I cannot refuse the king."

'"Then remember your promise," she said. "Mention me to no one."

'"Of course," he said. "I promised."

'"Yes you did," she said.

'So he went to the fair and watched the sport and the king's horses won every race. "Nothing could beat those creatures," said the man standing beside him. The farmer said, "Even my wife could run faster than that." The man turned to the one next to him and repeated the words. And he to the man next to him and these words were carried by the crowd to the ears of the king.

'The farmer tried to take back what he had said, but the king's men were already on their way to fetch his wife.

'There was to be a different kind of race.

'"I see you are carrying a heavy handicap," said the king when she was brought before him. The woman pleaded that the contest be put off until after the birth. He shook his head. She appealed to the crowd. "Help me," she cried.

'They turned away.

'"Kill me instead," the farmer begged, but it was too late for that. The race was on. At the start the horses strained while she stood still. Then they were off. Neck and neck they ran, a step, a stride, a gallop, a blur of brown and white, nostrils flaring, snorting in the air and with one last effort she crossed the line first and there she brought into the world a boy and a girl. Then she began to change.

'"Call yourselves men? You who watched and did nothing! I curse you." She reared up, her limbs now a hail of hooves clattering down over their heads. "You who stood there and said nothing! I curse you. Dumb animals! I curse you." Now the bit was between her teeth. "Know who I am! I am Macha!" screamed the nightmare. "You who once fell on your knees before me and my kind! Who ride our backs without a thought for all we have to bear! I curse you, the men of Ulster, to suffer the birth pangs of a woman whenever you are vulnerable and need help. I curse you for nine generations."

'Then all the men fell to the ground clasping their bellies and groaning as if they were fit to burst.'

'Enough of these labour pains, this ancient foreplay,' cried the oldest midwife, adding wood to the fire. 'It's time for the birth. I was there. I saw it all'.

Her siblings' eyes widened.

'It was spring when they came out of the sky – a flock of strange birds, pecking, pecking at the ground. With all the king's power he could not scare them away. Peck, peck they went, eating up the earth, devouring the crops, destroying the orchards. Wherever they descended, the land was laid waste and those that survived left scavenging for roots and berries.

'And through that desolate landscape rode King Conchobar and his men, always watching the sky, always one step behind.'

'Sister,' cried the middle one. 'You start your story too late and miss out the most important part.

'A year before, to that very day, the birds first came. I see a mayfly on the wing. A sensation seeking God, now jaded, eager to know how it feels to live for just one day and die. The mayfly circles above the great brown bull of Ulster and then lands upon the point of his right horn. At the back end, the other flies feast on the shit as it is carried off in silent ceremony and spread across the high king's fields. In one day the barley breaks through the earth and rises.

'The mayfly takes counsel with the great bull then bows and flies to the king's fortress where a feast awaits. The wedding feast of Dectera, the king's sister. There the bride lifts a cup to her lips. The mayfly dives in and for a moment is released from the monotony of immortality. Dectera swallows him down. Now inside her, he lives again and she begins to change – first a claw, then a beady eye, a beak and feathers. What was once soft is now sharp and she is soon on the wing with her new love. The bridal bed is empty. The bird has flown.

'The king searched for Dectera for a whole year before the birds came pecking at his door and as desperately as he had followed her, he now followed them with his men into the forest as darkness fell.

'The king sent his great champion, Conall the Victorious, and his great complainer, Bricriu of the Bitter Tongue, to search for a place to shelter that night. All they found was an old tumbledown house, with a donkey that had seen better days tied outside. The door opened and an old couple smiled and told them to bring their companions, as they were welcome to whatever they had. The two warriors returned to the king and told him all they had seen. "That is no place for the likes of us," said Bricriu spitting on the ground. "If they are generous enough to offer what little they have," said the king, "then we will not be mean enough to refuse it." But when they followed Conall and Bricriu back to the spot of the half-ruined house it was gone and in its place was a great mansion, streaming with light. Outside, untethered, stood a mighty mare stamping the ground. Then a scream pierced the air. The warriors gripped their swords, the door opened and out stepped a beautiful, shining, open-handed man. "Put down your weapons. You have nothing to fear here. That is just the sound of my wife bringing the new one into the world. I am Lugh. My element is light. All darkness has been long banished from this place."

'They entered the house and there was the greatest feast that anyone had ever seen. And they had seen a few. A herd of succulent pigs turned on spits. A flock of geese lay plucked and prepared on the table. A shoal of salmon swam in the boiling pots. And that was just for starters.

'"Great King," said Lugh, "This is the wedding feast delayed." Then there beside him was the face everyone knew, Dectera, and in her arms a new-born babe, a boy, who shone like his father.'

The youngest midwife sneered.

'You and your gods. You wrap up your propaganda in poetry and expect us to swallow it whole, when we all know what really happened.

'Sure there was a flock of birds, but it was winter. There was no disappearance, for I saw her with my own eye. Dectera driving the king's chariot into the dark forest where in that house brother and sister lay together. Then she was growing big and he married her off to some dupe but her husband was kind and then, ashamed, she killed that child she was carrying. But soon another life was growing inside her: her husband's son. His father was not a god, but a man as you know well.'

Then the three sisters cackling above the crackle of the fire turned on each other, screaming and hissing.

The eldest raised her hand. 'Listen,' she said. 'There is another quarrel happening. The men of Ulster cannot decide who will raise the child.'

Sencha, the judge, said, 'I will raise him as my own, so that he will be able to mediate and settle all disputes.'

'Disputes!' cried Blaí Briugu. 'I'll give you a dispute! The boy should come with me. I have great wealth and he will never want for anything.'

'A lad needs more than riches,' interrupted Fergus, the old king. 'He needs warmth and wisdom and I have an abundance of both.'

'All the words in the world are on my tongue,' said Amairgin, the poet, 'I would bring him up to speak like a king.'

The boy seemed to be delighted by all of them and it was decided that each would play their part. He was to be a man made by many and cherished by all. They named him Setanta.

As they left, the mare was gone but her two new-born steaming foals, the Grey and the Saingainn, were already standing tall. 'These are the mighty Macha's gifts to my son,' said Lugh, 'to be his constant companions in the world.' The boy, already growing fast, jumped onto the Grey's back and was off. The warriors raced to their chariots but he had already disappeared into the distance.

The hound howled. The three sisters fell silent and looked down. 'Perhaps,' said the youngest, 'it is this dog who really knows the truth.'

'Why should not such an extraordinary child have three fathers?' asked the middle one. 'A man, a king and a god?'

'Who cares about beginnings anyway?' said the oldest one, whetting the knife. 'What matters in the end, is the end, and we all know we will be there for that.'

She scratched the hound behind its ear, and then, with one easy movement, slit its throat.

2

THREE HOUNDS

Some things are forbidden, even to warriors and kings.

Each of the Ulster men had a demand or prohibition placed upon them – a *geis* – what they could never or should always do. This taboo was personal to them and its power went beyond duty. It was the law of the land.

Blaí Briugu was the richest man in the north and it was his *geis* to sleep with any woman who came unaccompanied to his house. Desire when demanded can become a pain, and Blaí Briugu had grown exhausted with pleasing the bored wives of warriors and tired of fighting their irate husbands.

One day, Brig Bretach, the wife of Celtchar mac Uthechar, came alone to his house. Both knew what this meant. He was reluctant. She was insistent. That night he fulfilled his obligation to her satisfaction. Her husband soon heard. Well, she was not going to keep something like that quiet and Celtchar, the younger man, pursued Blaí Briugu all the way into the sanctuary of the royal court at Emain Macha.

There, two kings, Conchobar and Fergus, were playing a game of chess. Castles had been defended and defeated, horses ridden out and brought down. Many pawns had already been sacrificed in pursuit of victory. Now, Conchobar's dark queen was leading Fergus's red king into a trap.

It was a move his mother had made many years before.

She had been the most beautiful woman in the land and Fergus wanted her. But she was not easy for the taking, even by a king.

She already had a son who was seven years old.

'Marry me,' said Fergus.

'On one condition,' she said.

'Whatever you desire is yours,' he said.

'Whatever?' she said.

'Anything,' he said. 'I am the king.'

'I want my son to be king after you,' she said.

'I would be proud if he were,' said Fergus.

'But what if another woman were to come along and took your fancy and you had your own child with her?'

'There are no other women as beautiful as you,' he said.

'I know that while men speak with their mouths today, tomorrow they act with other parts,' she said. Fergus smiled, for he was said to have been as well equipped as one of Macha's mighty stallions.

'How will I prove my words to you then?' he asked.

'Let my son be king for just one year so that all might see his destiny. Then the kingdom handed back to you my dear.'

He smiled at her and said, 'What is a year in the life of a great king?' and the boy, Conchobar, was placed upon the throne. Under his mother's guidance, he was a most generous ruler and Fergus did not notice for he was busy with his bride. When the year was up, he went to reclaim his crown, but the warriors of Ulster said, 'You treat us like your mistress. We are at the mercy of the whims of your desire. Let the crown stay with the one who bought it, not with the one who gave it away.'

Then a civil war raged across the land and the boy king won this as well. So Fergus lost his realm and the woman who had taken it, but finally a peace was made between the old king and the new.

Conchobar picked up the dark queen at the very moment that Blaí Briugu burst into the hall, pleading for the king's protection. No sooner were these words out of his mouth, than Celtchar raced in, flung his spear and Blaí Briugu's insides sprayed across the wall, the chess pieces were sent flying and the game of strategy became a bloody battlefield.

Conchobar was not pleased. Not only had the hospitality of his court been defiled, but the game he was about to win had been upset. Celtchar fled south and was exiled there.

One day, Fergus came with word from the king. 'Conchobar says that you can return if you rid Ulster from its three great pests: the Mouse Brown and Horny Skin mac Dedad.'

'That is only two pests,' said Celtchar.

'There's always three in the end,' said Fergus.

Now the Mouse Brown was a whelp of a hound that a widow had found in the hollow of a tree and had raised until it was grown.

For her kindness, the hound had killed her sheep, her cows, her son and then the widow herself.

The Mouse Brown lived in the Glen of the Great Sow and every night it terrorised the countryside and every day it slept. Celtchar went into the forest, cut down an alder tree, trimmed it, hollowed it out, boiled it in honey, herbs and grease and that night went to the cave of the Mouse Brown and waited for it to return.

In the morning as the Mouse Brown approached, it sniffed the air, saw the log lying there and then sank its teeth deep into it. With that, Celtchar thrust his arm through the hollow and into the mouth of the Mouse Brown, down its throat and pulled out its heart.

One down.

Now Horny Skin mac Dedad was as deadly as the Mouse Brown, but he was a man and would not be so easily fooled. For many months he had laid waste the land of Ulster and not a spear or sword could harm him. 'If we cannot flatten him,' said Celtchar, 'then we will flatter him.'

Celtchar went to meet Horny Skin with his daughter Niam who came armed not with weapons but with words. 'Is it true?' she asked, 'that you have killed a hundred Ulster warriors?'

'And more,' he said.

'How many more?' she asked.

'A hundred more,' he said.

'Then you are worth a hundred, hundred more than any Ulster man,' she said.

'And you are beautiful,' he said.

'And you are big and brave and handsome,' she said. One thing led to another and that night, as they lay together, she said, 'While a woman likes a man to be tough, she also likes him to be tender some of the time.'

'Women!' he said.

'Men!' she said. 'They can be so thick skinned.'

'Not I,' he said.

'Oh?' she said. 'I thought nothing could get through to you.'

'Almost nothing,' he said.

'Almost?' she said.

'Well, if someone were to thrust red-hot iron spits into the soles of my feet that would hurt,' he said. And they both laughed.

The next night Niam put sleeping herbs in his cup and held him close, as her father came and hammered red-hot iron spits through the soles of his feet and into his marrow and then cut off the head of Horny Skinned mac Dedad.

This great head was buried and the warriors of Ulster came with rocks and stones and built a burial mound over it.

A year passed and two cowherds were resting against that mound when they heard a sound coming from inside. They began to dig and found that the head was gone and in its place there were three whelps – a dun hound, a speckled hound and a black hound. Celtchar took the three pups, tucked them beneath his cloak and rode away. He hadn't travelled long when he came to Mac Da Thó's hostel and gave him the speckled hound as a gift to guard the greatest welcome to be found in Ireland.

The dun hound, he gave to Culann, the smith, in appreciation of all the horses shod and all the weapons forged.

The black hound he kept for himself, and it became his most beloved and constant companion. Years later, when Celtchar was away, his hound escaped and laid waste the land. No one could catch him and those who tried were ripped to pieces. When Celtchar returned, his hound came bounding towards him, jumped up and licked his face. Celtchar tickled him behind the ear and then thrust his spear into his heart and the third great pest of Ulster was slain.

3

THE
WONDER SMITH

One day King Conchobar saw a curious sight. On the playing fields of Emain Macha, a hundred and fifty boys were at one end of the green, while at the other, a single boy, Setanta, stood. They were playing the hole game, as boys do, but with different rules. The crowd of boys roared and ran at the one. Each tried to get their ball into the hole that Setanta was defending. No one succeeded. Then the positions were reversed. The hundred and fifty defended the hole while Setanta darted across the field, easily getting his ball past them and into the hole.

'Come and see this, Fergus!' cried the king. They watched as the hundred and fifty went to strip the clothes from Setanta, yet when the mud and the grass settled, it was they who stood there naked.

And the old king and the new king laughed, as they hadn't since they themselves were boys.

'He will be a mighty warrior,' said Fergus.

'Like his uncle,' said Conchobar.

'Like his foster father,' said Fergus.

'Like my father,' cried the boy, running towards them and embracing both.

'Now Setanta,' said Conchobar, 'Give those poor boys back their clothes.'

'In a while,' he said. 'Let's give everything a good airing first.'

'Now!' said Fergus. 'Then come with us to the feast at the blacksmith's forge.'

'I can't come yet for they are still playing and I don't want to spoil the game.'

'Well, we can't wait,' said the king.

'No need,' said Setanta. 'I will come along later.'

'You do not know the way,' said Fergus. 'I will follow in your chariot tracks,' shouted the boy running back to his companions.

The feast at Culann's forge was energetic and mostly edible and when their bellies were full the host asked the king, 'Are all your men inside?'

'Yes', said the king looking around. 'Why?'

'Well,' said Culann, 'I have a ferocious hound, born out of a burial mound, which guards the hall at night. While it is a pet to me, to every other man it is a beast that will tear them limb from limb.'

'Let loose your hound,' said Conchobar. 'For all are safe inside.'

Culann released his dun hound and this savage dog sniffed a circuit of the stronghold then settled down at its gate.

Back at Emain Macha, the game was over and Setanta was on the road, following the tracks of the chariots. With his club, he shortened the way for himself by hitting a ball, then running ahead and catching it before it hit the ground. The journey passed quickly in this way and within no time at all, he was approaching the gates of Culann's forge.

Boy and hound saw each other at the same time. Setanta's first instinct was to tickle the dog under its chin. But as the hound bared its teeth, Setanta could see that its only instinct was to swallow him whole.

The savage creature raced towards him. Now it would have its feast.

Inside the hall, all heard the howl.

'The boy!' cried Conchobar, remembering at last.

The doors were thrown open and all the warriors ran outside. The boy was yelling and running towards the dog and he took his ball and struck it into its black gaping mouth. The dog fell and the boy seized it by its hind legs and bashed its brains out against the ground.

Fergus lifted the lad onto his shoulders and carried him into the hall, as all the others chanted his name.

'The dog!' cried Culann as he rushed outside to see what had become of his beloved hound. He returned in a rage. 'You take what is given to you, yet now you take what is not given to you. The one that protects, that safeguards my herds and my hall is gone. The hound that shortened the darkness of my long nights is dead. Where is my compensation for this?'

'Here,' said the boy, now standing before the smith. 'I will search the whole of Ulster until I find a whelp of his kind and then I will raise it to be a hound as fierce and fit for action. Until that time, I myself will take up his place and guard all that you hold dear.'

Setanta did not return with the king. Instead he became the hound, patrolling the darkness, howling at the night sky. His days were spent forged in the fire of the magic and the making of the blacksmith's art.

One night, Culann looked up and asked Setanta what he saw. 'Stars,' said the boy.

'Those are the sparks from the Wonder Smith's anvil,' said Culann. 'Let me tell you a tale of the Gobán Saor.

'The Gobán Saor was the great Smith of the Gods. He had a daughter called Anya and he was not happy about this. "Ochone!" he would say. "Why was I given all the skills of all the trades in the world, yet no one to pass them on to?"

'Coming down the road, was an equally unhappy woman. She had a son, a dreamy boy who would do nothing that she asked. On hearing each other's tale of woe, they decided to swap. But no matter how hard the Gobán Saor tried to teach his new son, the boy preferred just to sit under a tree and play tunes on the reed flute he had made. The boy grew and one day the Gobán decided what his son needed was a clever woman for a wife. He sent the word out and three girls arrived at his door. He showed the first the treasures of his forge. "There's good spending here," she said. "You could take handfuls out and there would still be plenty left."

"'It will not be you who will be taking out the handfuls," said the Gobán. "My son will have a wiser wife."

'When the second girl saw the treasure, she said "I'll put seven bolts and seven bars on the seven doors of your forge, so that it will never grow less."

"'It will not be you putting the bolts and the bars on the doors," said the Gobán. "My son will have a wiser wife."

'The third girl looked at his treasures and said, "Well, there is a lot here, but there's certainly room for more."

"'And how would the more be got?" asked the Gobán Saor.

"'Through craft and the art of bargaining," said the girl.

'The Gobán Saor grabbed a sheepskin off the shelf. "Show me your art."

'He asked a reasonable price for the skin but couldn't resist her clever talk and she got it off him for half. "Very good."

"'That's nothing," she said. "With a little more craft, I could have paid you the price, given you back the skin and still come out the richer."

"'I'd like to see that."

"'I bet you would, but I must be going now," said the girl. And she walked out of the door.

'When his son came home the Gobán Saor said, "Take this sheepskin and find the one who will give you both the skin back and the price of it." The son set off with the sheepskin over his shoulder and with his milk-white hound, the Failinis, at his side. To every girl he met he said, "I will sell this only to the one who will pay the price of the skin and give it back to me." But he got no offers, until one cold winter's day he met a girl at a well.

"'That's a great burden you seem to be carrying," she said.

"'Yes," he said. "I must carry this skin until I meet someone who will give me the price of it, and give the skin back to me as well."

"'Sure, I could easily do that," she said. "Name your price."

'He did, and she gave him the price but she beat him down to half. Now the sheepskin was off his back the wind made him shiver.

'"Now give it back," he said, "as we agreed."

'"Yes, in a while," she said. She cut off the wool, wove a coat and gave him back the skin.

'"I could do with a coat," he said

'"How much will you pay?" she asked.

'Although the price was handsome, he was so cold now he was happy to give it.

'"You are the one my father seeks," he said, wrapping the warmth around himself.

'The milk-white hound raced home to the Gobán Saor and when the Gobán opened the door, he found his son in a fine new coat and the girl standing by his side.

'"What is your name?" asked the Gobán Saor.

'"Do you not know your own daughter?" she asked. "I am Anya."

'"Then come in and teach me all that you know," said the Gobán Saor.

'And it was that milk-white hound,' said Culann, 'that your father Lugh demanded as compensation for the killing of your grandfather and that dog, the Failinis, became his most beloved companion.'

From then on, to shorten each night, Culann told Setanta a tale of the Gobán Saor. When he had fulfilled his promise and raised a new hound fit to guard the blacksmith's forge, Culann said, 'Know that you will always be my hound, forever forbidden to eat the flesh of a dog. I give you a new name, Cúchulainn.

4

Pig
Feast

There were five great hostels in Ireland: the hostel of Da Derga among the men of Cualu, the hostel of Forgall Monach beside Lusk, the hostel of Da Reo in Brefne, the hostel of Da Choga in Westmeath and the hostel of Mac Da Thó in Kildare.

Each had seven doors and seven roads running up to them, each had seven cauldrons on seven fires, with an ox or a salted pig bubbling.

A warrior man off the road would thrust his flesh fork into a cauldron and whatever came out first he would eat and if nothing came out, then he would eat nothing.

Now Mac Da Thó's hostel was guarded by a remarkable speckled hound, one of the three born from the head in the burial mound. This dog knew no fear except what he placed in the hearts of the men who approached him. One day, two sets of messengers, one from Queen Medb and King Ailill, in Connacht and one from King Conchobar in Ulster, arrived at the hostel. Both were brought before Mac Da Thó who had the habit of welcoming guests whilst still in his bed. The messengers from Connacht stepped forward first. 'We come to ask for your hound and in exchange our king and queen offer you three hundred milch cows and a chariot pulled by the two fastest horses in the province.'

'We too come for the hound,' said the messengers of Ulster, 'and our king offers you the same and his friendship besides.'

For three days Mac Da Thó did not speak or sleep, trying to weigh up which deal would be the least worst, for to pick one as friend would mean having the other as foe. Then his wife came. 'Eat, husband!' she said.

'I cannot,' he said, 'for I am caught between a hawk and a wolf. If I let one have the hound, the other shall surely have me.'

'Then,' said his wife, 'why not give him to them both?' Mac Da Thó ate and drank his fill and went to where the messengers of Connacht were waiting.

'After much deliberation', he said. 'I have decided to give the hound to your king and queen. Ask them to come and collect him and I will hold a great feast in their honour.'

Relieved, the messengers returned to Connacht. Then Mac Da Thó went to the messengers of Ulster and said, 'I have decided to give the hound to your king. Ask him to come and I will hold a great feast in his honour.' The messengers returned to Ulster.

A month later, the King and Queen of Connacht and the King of Ulster, with their companies of warriors, arrived at exactly the same time at Mac Da Thó's hostel. He welcomed them warmly but they eyed each other suspiciously. For three hundred years they had been at war with one another and many carried the scar from it.

'Let the pig be killed,' cried Mac Da Thó. Then a feast was laid and sixty oxen dragged a cart in and on it a great pig that for seven years had been fed by three-score milch cows.

'The pig is good,' said Conchobar.

'How shall we divide it?' asked Ailill.

'By force of argument,' said Bricriu of the Bitter Tongue. 'The one who makes the strongest case for being the greatest warrior should carve the meat.' All were agreed and the contest began.

'I have slain many of your warriors, Conchobar!' cried Senlaech Aech. 'The pig belongs to me.'

'It was I who slew your brother,' said Munremur mac Gerrcind. 'The pig is mine.'

'And I slew yours and your father too,' said Cet mac Mágach, the champion of Connacht, reaching for the carving knife.

'Wait,' said Lóegaire. 'You have not yet faced us all.'

'Ah, but I have faced you, my lad, at the border, many moons ago. And took chariot and horse from you and in exchange left a spear through your thigh.'

Lóegaire sat down. 'Anyone else?' asked Cet.

'Yes,' said Angus, son of Hand-wail. 'I am a better warrior than you.'

'Well, let us hope you are a better warrior than your father,' said Cet. 'For I was the one who gave him his name when he cast a spear at me, and I returned it. I can still hear the sound as his hand went flying through the air.'

Angus sat down.

Cet looked around. 'Are there no others to challenge me?'

'Yes,' said Eógan mac Durthact. 'I say you are not fit to cut the pig.'

'I have seen you before,' said Cet. 'In front of your house when I took a herd of cattle off you and when you came to take them back, I took that eye out of your head.'

Eógan sat down.

Then Menn, son of Sword-heel stood up. 'Sit down,' said Cet. 'It was I who christened your father when I cut off one of his heels. I will not face the son of a nickname.'

Menn sat down.

'Well, you have not given me my name,' said Celtchar mac Uthechar with his faithful black hound at his side.

'No,' said Cet. 'I have given you much more than that. When I came to your house and the alarm was raised, you and your people came for me but my spear was swift and it tore through your loins and burst your balls so now you wet yourself like the babies you will never father.'

Celtchar sat down.

'He seems to be sharpening that tongue with his knife,' muttered Bricriu admiringly.

Then Conchobar's son, Cúscraid the Stutterer stood up and struggled to speak. 'Save your words,' said Cet. 'When you made your first raid upon us, I killed a third of your men and so that you would always keep my name upon your lips, I made you a new tongue with the point of my spear.'

Cúscraid sat down.

Cet looked around. All were silent now. He raised the knife and then one of the seven doors of the hostel opened and in walked Conall the Victorious. 'Ah! A feast!' he cried. 'And who will you be giving the knife to carve the pig?'

'I will be carving it myself,' said Cet.

'Yourself?' said Conall laughing. 'Surely that's a big beast for such a little lad.'

'I am no lad,' said Cet.

'Well you were, when I last met you and your brother and whipped both your skinny arses all the way back to that darling queen of yours. Apologies for the language ma'am,' he said, bowing to the darling queen in question.

'Since that time I haven't gone for one day without slaying a Connacht man or slept one night without the head of a Connacht man as my pillow.'

'Well, if only my brother, Analn mac Matach, was here tonight, then we would both show you who was the better man,' said Cet.

'But he is here,' said Conall. He took Analn's head from his bag, threw it at Cet's chest and the blood splattered across his face.

Cet sat down.

Conall took the knife and sang to himself as he carved the pig, consuming the tail as he went. When the men of Connacht saw their portion, they were not pleased. Conall had given them no more than a quarter of the pig. 'Let me give you some more,' said Conall as he took the pig's arse and added it on their plate. Then the whole place erupted. The Connacht men grabbed their swords and a great battle ensued. One thousand four hundred men were slain that night. Seven streams burst through the seven doors and the seven roads became seven red rivers of blood.

Mac Da Thó let loose his speckled hound to see which side the dog himself would choose and he joined the Ulster men. As the hound snapped at Medb's and Ailill's heels, they jumped into their chariot and fled. 'Have the hound!' cried Mac Da Thó after them. 'He's yours!' That hound followed them until the queen, with a throw of her spear, split him in two and then set his head upon a yew tree and that place has been named after him ever since.

So in the end no one got to keep the hound and Mac Da Thó went back to welcoming anyone who came to his hostel and he didn't need a guard dog now.

The story of the slaughter was enough to keep everyone well behaved after that.

5

A Call
to Arms

When Cúchulainn returned from the blacksmith's forge, having raised a hound as fierce as he had promised, he heard Cathbad the Seer say, 'Any lad who takes arms today, though his life will be short, his name will live long on the lips of men.'

Cúchulainn went to his uncle, the king. 'Cathbad has said that today is the day I should take arms,' he said.

'There is no wiser head in the land than his,' said Conchobar and he gave the boy two spears, a sword and a shield. Cúchulainn shattered them into shards and splinters.

The king gave him another set, and another and another. Each ended in the same way. Finally Conchobar gave him his own weapons and they did not break. 'These will do,' cried the boy.

Then Cathbad entered the king's hall and asked, 'Why is that boy carrying arms?'

'Because you told him to,' said the king.

'I may be old,' said Cathbad, 'but it will be a while yet before I don't know the difference between a boy, a man and a warrior.'

The king looked at Cúchulainn. 'Is this some prank little one?'

'No prank,' said Cúchulainn. 'I heard Cathbad say that if a lad takes arms today, though his life be short, his story will be long. Better to live just one day as a warrior and be praised for all time as a hero.'

'As you speak as someone who has taken arms,' said Cathbad, 'now take a chariot.'

After seventeen chariots were brought and Cúchulainn had reduced each to fragments, Conchobar called on his charioteer, Lubar mac Riangabra, to prepare his own chariot and harness his own horses. The chariot did not buckle beneath Cúchulainn. 'This one suits me well,' he said.

'Good lad,' said Lubar mac Riangabra. 'Now let the horses be turned out to grass again.'

'Not before I salute my comrades at play,' said Cúchulainn. So Lubar drove the chariot to the playing fields where the boys were amazed to see that Cúchulainn had taken arms so young. Lubar began to turn the chariot towards the meadows, but Cúchulainn asked, 'Where does that great road ahead lead?'

'To the lookout ford in Sliab Fúait,' said Lubar, 'where a single warrior watches and stands guard against our enemies and soothes poets as they come and go from Ulster so they will sing great praise songs in our honour, rather than curse us under their breath.'

'Who guards the ford today?' asked Cúchulainn.

'Conall Cernach, the one they call the Victorious, for he is the greatest warrior in Ulster.'

'Onward to the ford then driver,' cried Cúchulainn.

'The king will be wanting his chariot back,' said Lubar.

'My uncle has given me this chariot,' said Cúchulainn. 'To the ford if you please.'

At the ford, they found Conall waiting with his horse, the Dewey Red. 'You are mighty young to have taken arms,' he said.

'And you are mighty old to be guarding this ford all on your own,' said Cúchulainn. 'Let me lift the burden from you. I will keep watch today.'

Conall began to laugh. He liked the swagger of the lad, but said, 'It is different games you would have facing real fighting men than with the boys on the playing fields of Emain Macha.'

'Don't I know it,' said Cúchulainn. 'And if I cannot guard this ford, then I will ride to the borderlands and meet those fighting men.'

'You will not go alone,' said Conall.

'I will,' said Cúchulainn picking up a stone as big as his fist and firing it at Conall's chariot, the force breaking its yoke.

Conall was furious, but Cúchulainn cried, 'Why wait for your foes to come to you when you can go to them?'

As they travelled southwards, Lubar all the while tried to persuade Cúchulainn to turn back. But he replied, 'you are just a lazy loon. Enjoy our first adventure!'

'I hope it is not our last,' said Lubar.

They came to the mountain of Shab and from there, Lubar pointed out all the hills and plains and strongholds of the province; Tailltiu, Knowth, the Brug of Aengus mac Oc and the stronghold of the sons of Nechtan Sceine. 'Are those the men of whom its said they have killed more Ulstermen than are alive today?'

'The very same,' said Lubar, hoping to scare the lad.

'Then we will go there next,' said Cúchulainn.

'No,' said Lubar, 'it is too dangerous.'

'You will go dead or alive,' said Cúchulainn.

'Alive I will go and dead I will be coming back,' said Lubar.

They rode on to the stronghold of the sons of Nechtan Sceine and Cúchulainn stepped out of the chariot, yawned and fell asleep on the green.

Foill, the eldest son of Nechtan, came charging out. 'Driver! Do not unharness those horses.'

'No indeed,' said Lubar. 'I'm just taking this young 'un round to see the sights, just play acting that he's been given arms today.'

Cúchulainn woke up to these words. 'Play acting?' he cried. 'I'm a warrior ready for action!'

'Ready for a prompt and violent death,' Lubar muttered under his breath.

'If he says he's ready, then he's ready,' said Foill mac Nechtan.

'Thank you,' said Cúchulainn.

'But he's just a boy,' said Lubar.

'Better the boy become a corpse today than return as a man to irritate me tomorrow,' said Foill, turning to fetch his arms.

'Good,' said Cúchulainn.

'That's not good,' said Lubar.

'Why not?' asked Cúchulainn.

'Well,' said Lubar. 'It is well know that Foill mac Nechtan is invulnerable to the point or edge of any weapon.'

'What about balls?' asked Cúchulainn.

'Balls?' repeated Lubar.

'Yes. I have an iron ball,' said Cúchulainn. 'How does he fare with balls?'

'This is not well known,' said Lubar.

'Good,' said Cúchulainn and as Foill rushed yelling towards him, Cúchulainn threw the ball and it hit him in the forehead, taking his brains out through the back of his skull. No sooner had he fallen, than out of the stronghold came Tuachall, the second son of Nechtan.

'Good!' cried Cúchulainn.

'Bad!' cried Lubar.

'Why bad?' asked Cúchulainn.

'Well,' said Lubar, 'it is well known that Tuachall mac Nechtan can only be killed by the first blow or not at all.'

'Good!' cried Cúchulainn again.

'Good?' repeated Lubar.

'Yes. Well we don't want to waste any time,' said Cúchulainn. And with that, he let loose the Venomous, Conchobar's great spear, and it pierced Tuachall's chest and took his heart out through the back of his ribs. No sooner had he fallen, than out of the stronghold came Fainulae, the third son of Nechtan, running towards them. He challenged Cúchulainn to fight him in water where no foot could touch the bottom.

'Don't accept,' muttered Lubar.

'I accept,' cried Cúchulainn. Lubar shook his head.

'What's the matter now?' asked Cúchulainn.

'Well', said Lubar, 'it's well known that Fainulae mac Nechtan is as swift as a swallow over water.'

'Well at least it won't be a walkover like the others,' said Cúchulainn.

But it was, as Cúchulainn took off the third son's head with one stroke of Conchobar's sword without even getting wet. He held the head as the body was carried away by the current.

They set light to the stronghold of the sons of Nechtan and then Cúchulainn tied the heads of the three sons to the front of his chariot. 'Now,' he said, 'where can we find some more trophies?'

'More!' cried Lubar.

'Well, we can't just go back with a few old heads,' said Cúchulainn. 'It is my first day of taking arms after all!'

'Of course not. That would be ridiculous,' said Lubar in a tone that Cúchulainn did not quite understand.

'What about those skinny cows over there?' asked Cúchulainn.

'Those are deer,' said Lubar.

'And are they worth having?' asked Cúchulainn.

'I guess,' said Lubar. 'But this chariot will be too slow to catch them.'

'Dead or alive?' asked Cúchulainn.

'What?' asked Lubar.

'Is there more glory in bringing them back dead or alive?' asked Cúchulainn.

'Alive,' said Lubar.

'Should we have kept the brothers alive?' asked Cúchulainn, concerned now.

'No. They're better off dead,' said Lubar.

'Oh good,' said Cúchulainn. He jumped down from the chariot, ran swiftly through the trees and brought back two great stags. He tied them, alive, to the front of the chariot. As they headed back to Emain Macha, they came across a flock of swans. 'I think we should have some of those white things too,' said Cúchulainn and with two stones, he stunned twenty-four of the birds and brought them down ahead of the racing chariot. 'Could you pick them up as we drive past?' asked Cúchulainn.

'Not really,' said Lubar, 'for if I try, I fear that either the chariot wheels or those stags' antlers will cut me to pieces.'

'You're not a very good warrior, are you?' said Cúchulainn.

'No,' said Lubar. 'But I am a very good charioteer.'

'Oh go on! Try!' said Cúchulainn. 'It is our first day together. Do it for me. I will gaze at the horses so they hold a regular pace and I will gaze at the stags so they hold their heads low.' As the chariot raced past, Lubar reached down and snatched up the swans. Cúchulainn tied them, alive, to the front of the chariot. Lubar, shaking and sweating, slumped back into his seat.

At Emain Macha, Leborcham, the king's messenger – so fleet of foot, she could run the length of Ireland in one day – was looking towards the setting sun. When she saw them approaching, she cried out:

> 'A fiery chariot comes.
> White birds flapping.
> Splashed red.
> Our enemy's heads hanging.
> Two stags leaping.
> A furious boy,
> Bathed in blood and gold,
> Thunders across the plain.'

'How do we stop him?' asked the king.

Leborcham had an idea. She and all the women of Ulster stripped off and walked out naked to greet the boy. Cúchulainn's embarrassment, like everything else about him, was excessive. He closed his eyes and Lubar brought the horses to a halt. Then the women seized the boy, his eyes still tightly shut and they plunged him into a barrel of water. It exploded from his heat. Then they plunged him into a second barrel, which bubbled and boiled and into a third, which was just right. Cúchulainn blushed red from the crown of his head to the soles of his feet as the women dried and dressed him in fresh clothes.

That night, the boy took his place on Conchobar's lap and as the king stroked his hair, he fell fast asleep.

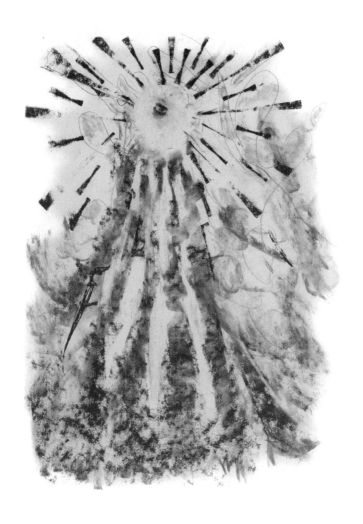

6

THE STORYTELLER'S
DAUGHTER

Conchobar and the warriors of Ulster were gathered in the hall of the saga slayers before Fedlimid, the king's storyteller. He waited until all were silent and then began his tale.

'In a land of ice there stood a tower without window or way out. Inside twelve women weaned and watched over their charge. She was a daughter of darkness who had never known the light. Her father, a great one-eyed god by the name of Balor, had heard a prophecy.

'If his daughter ever bore a child, then that child would grow up to kill him. So he kept her locked up in the world of women with no knowledge of men. Yet as she grew, she dreamed of things she could not know – of creatures like her, yet strangely different.

'A lad named Cian heard of the tower and of the girl and he liked a challenge. So one stormy night, he disguised himself as a woman and went knocking. Some story about being lost and cold and hungry gained him entry. In truth he was prettier than any of the women. There was only one spare bed with the girl up top. "Would you mind sharing?"

'"Not at all," Cian said.

'What a night they had. If she thought the creatures in her dreams were strange, they were nothing compared to this.

'In the morning he left her not just with many questions, but with something else. A child was coming. She tried to hide it, but it's hard to disguise something like that, especially from twelve old fusspots.

'When the baby was born, her father tried to kill it, but even he knew that's not how this story was going to end.

'When the boy, Lugh, grew into a man he went to find his father and at last he was standing at the gates of the High King's hall.

'"Who are you?" asked the gatekeeper.

'"I am a builder," said Lugh.

'"We have a builder already," said the gatekeeper.

'"I am a smith," said Lugh.

'"We have a smith already," said the gatekeeper.

'"I am a champion," said Lugh.

'"We have a champion already," said the gatekeeper.

'"I am a harper," said Lugh.

'"We have a harper already," said the gatekeeper.

'"I am a poet," said the Lugh.

'"We have a poet already," said the gatekeeper.

'"I am a physician," said Lugh.

'"We have a physician already," said the gatekeeper.

'"I am a magician," said Lugh.

'"We have a magician already," said the gatekeeper.

'"I am a warrior," said Lugh.

'"We have many warriors," said the gatekeeper.

'"Ask your king," said Lugh, "whether he has any man who is the master of all these arts."

'When the gatekeeper brought these words to those inside, Cian said, "That sounds like my son" and welcomed him in.

'But this is not the story of the birth of a son,' said Fedlimid, the storyteller, 'it is the story of the death of a father. One day when Cian was out riding on his own, he saw the three sons of Tuireann. They were of his tribe but a blood feud existed between his family and theirs. Spotting some pigs, he struck himself with a hazel wand, changed into a sow, and lost himself amongst the herd. Brian, Tuireann's eldest son, saw what he had done and struck his brothers with a rod of rowan and they turned into two fierce hounds. He let them go. Cian stopped rooting in the ground and ran towards a wooded grove. Brian flung his spear and brought him down.

'"Do you not know me?" cried Cian.

'"A pig that speaks Irish! Now there's a thing!" said Brian. "Yes. We know you well."

'"Then let me change into my right shape."

'"Gladly," said Brian. "I would much rather kill a man than a pig."

'Cian became a man again.

'"Hah!" he said. "If you had killed me in the shape of a pig, then the blood price for my life would have been a pig, but kill me now as I am, a man, then the blood price of my death will be your death."

'"But who will know if we kill you?" asked Brian.

'"The weapons you carry will cry out the story of my death," said Cian.

'"Then we will not use these weapons, but the stones of the earth to kill you."

'And the three brothers picked up stones and rocks from the ground and pelted Cian until he was an unrecognisable mass of flesh.

'They buried him, but the earth, not wanting to be implicated in his murder, brought Cian to the surface again. Seven times they buried him before the earth accepted his body.

'When his father did not return, Lugh went searching for him. Lugh listened to the trees bending in the wind, the water rushing over rocks, the mountains being worn away by the rain until he found the spot where his father had been killed. The earth told him all that had happened. Lugh dug deep and then raised a great burial mound over the remains.

'He returned to the king's court and there among all the warriors, sat the three sons of Tuireann. Lugh shook the chain of attention of the court, and all listened. "I have a question for each of you," he said. "Who do you love most?"

All answered, "Our kith and kin."

'"Who do you hate most?"

'"Those that would kill our kith and kin," they said.

'"And what price would you ask for such a killing?"

'The king spoke. "We all know the price for that."

'"My father is dead," said Lugh. "Killed at the hands of three who sit here. But I do not seek their death if they make themselves known; a different compensation will be asked."

'The three sons of Tuireann stood and asked, "What is the compensation that you seek?"

'"Three apples," said Lugh, "seven live pigs and the skin of a dead one; a spear; two steeds, one puppy dog and three shouts from a hill."

'"Is that all?" asked Brian.

'"I do not deem it too little a price," said Lugh.

'"You will not ask for more?" asked Brian.

'"No more," said Lugh.

'And the brothers pledged before the king and the company that they would bring back the compensation he asked. Lugh smiled.

'"The apples," he said, "are to be the colour of burnished gold; as big as the head of a month old child; taste of honey and are not diminished when eaten. The seven pigs must be killed at night and be alive again in the morning. The skin of the pig must be able to heal all wounds and stop all disease. The spear you have promised to bring is so fiery that it has to be kept in a cauldron of water lest it burn down the forests of the land. The two steeds must be as swift across water as they are on land. The puppy dog is the milk-white Failinis, the most ferocious hound on earth and you must give the three shouts from the hill of Midchain."

'The three brothers were worried now. They went to their father who said it was a just price for what they had done, but he gave them his blessing and each day looked for their safe homecoming.

'At length they returned and laid all the things that Lugh had asked for at his feet. He said, "Now, go to the top of Midchain's hill and when you make three shouts, the price will have been paid."

'As they climbed, Midchain, the guardian of the hill came yelling towards them, and he and Brian fought like two fierce wolves until Midchain fell. Then his three sons, Corc, Con and Aod, came running across the hill and there the sons of Midchain fought the sons of Tuireann and each drove their spears into the other until the sons of Midchain were dead and the sons of Tuireann barely living.

'"We must make our three shouts," said Brian.

"We cannot," said his brothers. But he lifted their heads and as blood flowed from their mouths they raised the three shouts. Brian was the only one left alive to return and he was already more in the next world than this.

'His father did all he could, yet knew it was not enough. Old Tuireann went to Lugh and asked to borrow the healing pigskin that his sons had brought.

'"I have lost two sons. Save the other one," he pleaded.

'Lugh looked at him and said, "I have lost a father. Three sons is the price that has to be paid."

'Tuireann buried Brian with his brothers and stood over the grave, "I was once a mighty warrior with three great sons but now their strength is no longer mine. Neither is the sun nor the sky nor the earth. All is gone now." And with that the father fell and joined his sons.

'That is the end of the first sorrow of storytelling,' said Fedlimid.

'What is the second?' asked the king.

'A man and a woman had four children, but the mother died and the father took a new wife. At first he was happy with his woman and she delighted in him but resented his children. As time went on, she wanted more of him for herself. One day, she asked her husband, "Who do you love most?" and he said, "My children." So she took to her bed for a year. He did not seem to notice. One day she took the children to the edge of a lake, struck each with a hazel wand, turned them into four swans, and cursed them to live in this form for nine hundred years.

'Then she went to their father and told him what she had done, and asked, "Who do you hate most?" And at last she got the attention she craved.

'The children flew away and when they finally returned to their own land, they found that their father's great house was now a ruin, overgrown by the forest, and a new queen ruled there. She heard about the swans that sang so sweetly and sent her men to catch them. But when the cage was brought to her, inside there were four ancient people looking back at her and in their eyes she saw the suffering of the whole world.

'And that is the end of the second sorrow of storytelling,' said Fedlimid.

'Please don't give us a third,' said the king.

That night, as the household slept, a great howl filled the hall, and the warriors rushed for their swords. All they found was Fedlimid's pregnant wife standing there.

'The sound came from inside me,' she said.

Cathbad, the king's seer, placed his hand upon her belly and closed his eyes. He smiled. 'She is beautiful.'

'It is a daughter,' said Fedlimid, squeezing his wife's hand.

'The most beautiful girl we will ever see, with golden locks, her cheeks aglow like foxgloves, green eyes that pierce the soul, and lips red like coral.'

But then his face changed as if a storm crossed it now. 'She will bring an epic of destruction into this world.

'Men will fight for her. Kings will kill for her. Armies will march for her; brother against brother; husband against wife; father against son. Wherever she goes, a grave will be dug, a headstone raised. She will be known as Deirdre, the daughter of tears.'

And before the night was out, a baby girl was born and the men would have killed her there and then, if King Conchobar hadn't placed her under his protection. He hid her away from the eyes of the world, raised by his trusted servant, Leborcham, and indeed she did grow into the most beautiful woman that Ulster had ever seen.

To protect her charge, Leborcham told the king that Deirdre had grown into an ugly woman. But one day he came and saw for himself that she was everything that he desired.

One winter's day, Deirdre watched as Leborcham skinned a calf and as the blood fell on the snow, a crow flew down to drink it.

'The man I want,' she said, 'will have hair as black as that crow, lips as red as that blood and skin as white as that snow.'

The crow looked back at her, relishing what was to come.

That night, she was woken by a beautiful song and for the first time in her life, she left where she had been kept and followed the sound until she came to the ramparts of the fortress. There, singing his warrior's cry, was a man whose hair was black, whose lips were red and whose skin was white. His name was Naoise and he was the king's nephew, one of the sons of Uisnech – three brothers so swift that they only hunted deer on foot, so sweet singing that any cow that heard them gave two-thirds more milk, so skilled with arms that if they set their backs against each other all the warriors in Ulster could not defeat them.

She looked at him and knew this was the man for her. Deirdre ran past him and at first he did not know her.

'Great is the young heifer that springs by me now,' he cried.

'Heifers are great,' she said, 'in a place where there are no bulls.'

Then he knew her. 'I hear you have the king of bulls at your call,' he said.

'Better a young bull like you than some old one,' she said.

The more she had been hidden, the more talk there had been about her, and although he could not take his eyes off her, he shook his head.

'Coward!' she cried as she grabbed his ears. 'Two ears of shame and mockery if you will not have me.' He protested, but it was too late. A *geis* was upon him. He was bound to her now.

He called his two brothers and they all fled Conchobar's court that night and headed south. But the king sent mercenaries to pursue them, so they sailed to another land and became warriors for another king.

All the while Deirdre was hidden away from men's eyes.

Conchobar sent his spy, Gelban, to track them down but just as Gelban put his eye to the crack in the door, Naoise poked it out with the point of his spear.

Even so, he returned to Conchobar's court with a smile upon his face. 'Better to be blinded at the sight of her than never to have seen her at all,' he said.

The king knew then that she was as beautiful as ever.

One day by chance the king whom the brothers now served glimpsed Deirdre and he also thought her fit for a king. So he sent them on increasingly dangerous and difficult missions but to his dismay they always returned in one piece. As time passed, her image burned itself ever more brightly into his mind and he gathered together his warriors to destroy the sons of Uisnech.

So they fled again and now Conchobar saw his chance.

He sent word to them that all was forgiven. Were they not his kith and kin? He did not want them to be killed in a foreign land. To honour his word he sent Fergus, the old king, as surety of safe passage and Fergus greeted the three brothers as if they were long lost sons. Deirdre did not trust Conchobar's words, but where else were they to go?

When they reached the shores of Ulster, Conchobar had laid on a great feast for Fergus alone, knowing that he was under a *geis* that forbade him to refuse such an invitation.

Deirdre and the sons of Uisnech rode on now, escorted by Fergus's son, Fiachra.

When they reached Emain Macha, they were greeted by the king with great ceremony and as Deirdre was taken away by the ladies, the brothers were led out onto the green where they were surrounded by the mercenaries of Eógan mac Derthact.

High on the ramparts stood Conchobar, watching and Deirdre was brought to him, her arms bound at her back.

Eógan let loose his spear at Naoise. Fiachra leapt into the air and threw both arms around Naoise, the point passed through him and Naoise was slain through the body of Fergus's son.

Then brother fought brother and father fought son, there on the green at Emain Macha.

Fergus arrived at dawn to see the bodies and the blood, the treachery and a prophecy fulfilled. But he knew that this was not a woman's doing, but a king's. He took a torch and set the fortress ablaze and with three thousand men went into exile to the land of Connacht to serve Conchobar's enemies, Queen Medb and King Ailill.

For a whole year Conchobar kept Deirdre by his side. In all that time she never smiled or raised her head, hardly ate or slept and each day he would ask her, 'Who do you love most?'

And she would say, 'the one with hair as black as a crow, with lips as red as blood, with skin as white as freshly fallen snow.'

At year's end he asked her, 'Who do you hate most?'

'You,' she said, 'and Eógan mac Derthact.'

'Then,' he said, 'you will live with Eógan for a year and we will see if you love me any more at the end.' So the next morning, Deirdre was led out to Eógan's chariot and there she sat between those who had killed the one she loved. As she looked up at them, Conchobar laughed. 'There you sit like a ewe eyeing up two rams.'

But Deirdre stood up, looked them both in the eye and let out a great cry. Conchobar recognised the howl he had heard before she was born. Then Deirdre threw herself from the chariot and she was shattered on the rocks below.

Conchobar knew that this was the end of the third sorrow of storytelling.

7

GARDENS
OF THE SUN

Cúchulainn had it all – the charm, the strength, the moves –
the women of Ulster seemed to talk of nothing else. It was said
that he had only three defects: he was too young, too brave and
too handsome.

The men of Ulster were worried. Wives, daughters, mothers,
even some of the warriors themselves had begun to swoon.
Something had to be done. A wife had to be found and quick.
Nine men were sent into each of the provinces of Ireland to
find someone suitable. Cúchulainn found none of their choices
suitable. He had his eyes set on the place where his father's
face shone brightest and where Forgall the Wiley had built his
fortress. With him there lived his daughter, Emer, who was said
to possess the six gifts: beauty, voice, sweet speech, handicraft,
wisdom and chastity. So Cúchulainn went awooing to the
gardens of the sun. On the day of his arrival, Emer was stretched
out on the ground looking up at the sky. Hearing the clatter of
hooves, the cracking of straps and the clanking of weapons, she
asked, 'What is coming this way?'

Her sister, Fial, said, 'I see two steeds alike in size, beauty and
speed: a grey with a look of lightning burning up the land and a
black with the power of thunder storming across the plain.'

'I am not interested in horses,' said Emer. 'What else do you see?'

'I see a chariot of wood with wheels of bronze and a strong
curved yoke of gold and two hard shafts as strong and straight
as spears.'

'I am not interested in chariots,' said Emer. 'What else do you see?'

'I see a beautiful crimson five-folded tunic fastened with a broach of inlaid gold.'

'I am not interested in fashion,' said Emer. 'What else do you see?'

'I see a man as beautiful as the setting sun. A ray of love burns through his look. His eyebrows as black as a charred beam, his eyes ablaze with fire.' Emer sat up. Now this was something she was interested in.

As he approached, she rose and turned to face him. 'May the path be smooth before you,' she said.

'And may you,' he said, 'never suffer harm or hurt.'

'Which way did you come?' she asked.

'Between the two mountains of wood,' he said.

'And from there?'

'That is easy to tell,' he said. 'From the cover of the sea, over the great secret of the Tuatha de Danann, through the foam of the horses of Macha, over the Morrigu's garden and the great sow's back, between a god and a man, over the marrow of a woman, between a boar and his dam, to the four corners of the world, over the great crime and the remnants of the great feast, between the big vat and the little vat, to the spot where we are standing now.' Flirting was different in those days.

'And where are you headed?' she asked.

Noticing her breasts, he said, 'I hope to journey on to the fair plain before me now, between the mountain of the sun and the mountain of the moon.' Flirting was not so different in those days.

'A noble daughter,' she said, 'has to be the flame of hospitality to all men, yet there are some places where they may not enter.'

'Even a man like me?' he asked.

'Especially a man like you,' she said.

'You don't even know me,' he said.

'So, then, what kind of man are you?' she asked.

'One raised by warriors and wise women, jokers and judges, poets and kings. I am fierce in might yet I am shelter for all the poor and weak who need my help.'

'You are very full of yourself,' she said.

'No,' he said, looking straight at her. 'I am full of the men and the women who have made me. And yet I need another to finish me.'

'Well then,' she said. 'A man may enter the plain that lies before you if he can leap over the three walls of my father's fortress in one bound and slay three times nine men with one blow, while leaving my three brothers unhurt and carry off my weight in gold.'

'I will take that as a yes, then,' he said.

But she could not give herself away and her father did not want her to marry this madman from the north. He was not foolish enough to say so, as he could see the light in his daughter's eyes.

Instead he said, 'The lad is not ready,' and turning to Cúchulainn, he said, 'Find the one they call the Shadow Catcher and if you survive that finishing school, then return to face me.'

As Forgall watched him go, to himself, he said, 'There are dangers and distractions for a young man in this world. He will not return.'

As Emer watched him go, to herself, she said, 'that is the man for me. I long for his return.'

As for Cúchulainn, his only thoughts were on what it was that lay beyond the horizon.

8

Shadow Lands

Cúchulainn was following the road of whispers between the cracks. Through the plain of ill luck, he entered the Shadow Lands.

There was word of the Shadow Catcher everywhere, but no sign anywhere.

'The Shadowy one is not here; travel on.'

'Over the next mountain.'

'How could anyone have trained all those great warriors?'

'A day – a week – a month – a year away.'

'Long dead.'

Then one day Cúchulainn found himself standing at the side of a rushing river and he was not alone.

Hungry-looking young warriors stood on the bank, watching him. 'Have you seen the one they call the Shadow Catcher?' he asked.

'Sure!' they said. 'Over there,' pointing to an island in the middle of the roaring waters.

'And how will I get there?'

'Oh, there's a bridge to cross over.'

'I am obliged to you,' said Cúchulainn.

The bridge seemed solid enough, but as soon as he stepped onto it, it became as narrow as the bristle on a boar's back and Cúchulainn toppled over into the water.

'Try again,' the other warriors cried encouragingly. He did and this time, the bridge became as short as a man's thumb and he was drenched again. 'You seem to be getting the hang of it now,' called out one of the young men. Cúchulainn stared at him hard and then raced towards the bridge. But as soon as he set foot on it, it became as slippery as an eel and Cúchulainn found himself in the river again. The young warriors could contain themselves no longer and began to laugh and to Cúchulainn, the one who had called out seemed to be laughing louder than the rest and he leapt at him. As the others chanted and cheered, the two of them rolled around on the ground like a pair of young hounds, each struggling to be top dog. Cúchulainn had never felt this strength in another before and all the while his young opponent winked and blew kisses at him until finally, disarmed and exhausted Cúchulainn began to laugh. 'I am Cúchulainn,' he said, offering his hand.

'I know who you are. The girls I meet speak of no one else. Close up, I can see what all the fuss is about.'

'You are a finer young buckeen I'm sure,' replied Cúchulainn with a wink.

'I am Ferdiad, son of Daman and those other young rascals over there are all brothers. Now at last I have a brother of my own.'

'Indeed you do,' said Cúchulainn. 'One as strongly bound to you now as if by blood.'

'Then, brother,' said Ferdiad, 'let me help you with that bridge. A tip for you. The next time you step on it, the middle will grow tall like the mast of a ship.'

'I'm much obliged to you, little brother,' said Cúchulainn.

'Oh, so it's little brother, is it, now?' Ferdiad sent Cúchulainn on his way with a kick to his backside. 'May the gods go with you.'

Cúchulainn jumped onto the bridge and as the middle rose, he leapt up like a salmon and seemed to shimmer like a god as he somersaulted through the air. He landed safely on the island.

There, perched on a branch in a great yew tree, was a little old woman with a staff of hazel wood in her hand. 'Where is he?' asked Cúchulainn.

'He's not at home today,' she said. 'Come back tomorrow.'

'I will wait,' he said.

'Very well,' she said, all the while smiling at him as he stood there. The day passed and the shadows lengthened. He was getting impatient and began to pace. 'Are you sure you don't want to come back tomorrow?' she asked.

'Yes,' he growled. 'Quite sure.'

'You see, I have been waiting many days now for him to fly back to me,' she said.

'He flies!' said Cúchulainn.

'Oh yes! Most birds fly,' she said.

'Bird?'

'Yes, my little pet crane. Where is he? I have been asking myself for days now,' she said.

'Birds!' cried Cúchulainn. 'I'm not interested in birds!'

'Wasn't your mother a bird at one point?' she asked.

'You leave my mother out of it,' he said.

'I'm looking for Scathach.'

'You should have said,' she said. 'You have found her.'

'Her!' he cried.

'Here!' she cried.

'But you are a woman,' he said.

'There's clearly no fooling you,' she said.

'I can't be trained by a woman,' he said.

'Did you not come out of a woman?' she asked. 'Or was it a bird? Or a hole in the ground? It's so hard to tell these days. Surely if one woman started you, another could finish you?'

'Now look you old bag of bones! Where can I find the one they call the Shadow Catcher?'

She jumped down from the branch of the tree and with one swift swipe of her staff, she wrong footed him and he fell on the ground in front of her.

'Please get up,' she said. 'My days of rejecting proposals from suitors are long gone.'

'Suitor,' spluttered Cúchulainn, 'I have come to be trained in the ways of warrior-hood.'

'Well I don't train just anybody,' she said.

'Anybody!' he cried. 'I am Cúchulainn of Ulster. My mother is the king's sister.'

'Well, I'm sure she will be missing you,' she said.

'Missing me!' Cúchulainn flew at her, grabbing her hair and placing the point of his spear to her heart.

'Do you not know I could kill you in the blink of an eye?' he screamed.

She, chuckling, threw her arms wide, embraced him and as she did so, Cúchulainn saw the spear pass through her body and all the while she kept his gaze.

'And did I blink?' she asked. 'Now put away that toy before you hurt yourself.'

Then she was off.

'Will you teach me?' he called after her.

She turned. 'What do you think I have been doing? Scratching my arse?'

'So, you will?' he said. She looked him up and down as if surveying some poor hopeless creature.

'I suppose we will have to work with what we have got,' she said. Cúchulainn began to smile. Scathach was now stony faced.

'Come back tomorrow,' she said. 'And remember to bring your manners with you.'

As he watched her disappear up the path, scattering hen feed as she went, Cúchulainn knew that his training had begun.

The next morning, Cúchulainn suddenly awoke to a sharp ringing in his head as if his skull was an iron bell and someone was using his brain as the clapper to make it sound. His vision blurred. At first he could make out two Scathachs standing above him. These soon became the one who had brought her staff down upon his head. 'If you dream your days away,' she said, 'one day there might be no reason to wake up.'

He followed her outside.

She seemed to dance across the ground, the sun, a golden ball rising into the sky as if at her command. 'Let's fight,' she said. He looked at his sword and then at her staff. She looked into his eyes. 'Remember yesterday,' she said. His eyes narrowed and he looked at the staff again. 'Good,' she said. 'You look ready for lesson two.' Then before he knew it, he was being assaulted everywhere at once and all the while she was whispering in his ear, 'If I wanted to I could chop your arm off, paralyse you, make you impotent.' But every time he tried to strike at her, she was not there.

On the third day, he was up before her and waited outside. He waited for her all day but she did not come.

The next day, there she was again. 'Why did you not speak to me yesterday?' she asked.

'You were not here,' he said.

'I was,' she said.

'I did not see you,' he said.

'Did you not look at the bark of the tree? Did you not see the green of the grass? Did you not feel the solidness of the ground beneath your feet? Or hear the wind? That's where I was waiting for you.'

He did not know what to say.

'No matter, today you will have to work twice as hard,' and she threw him a spear. 'Now bring me down.'

She walked away and turned.

He flung the spear. She closed her eyes and caught it and released her staff and as he leapt into the air he heard it whistle past his ear. 'Hah, she has missed,' he thought. But then he realised that he was not falling back to earth. He looked down.

She was gazing up at him.

'Avoid the obvious,' she said. 'If you are going to kill someone, do not bore them to death. Have the courtesy to at least take them by surprise.'

Cúchulainn then could see that her staff held his shadow pinned to the ground.

'Aim for the shadow, for that's where our weakness lies.'

She kept him hovering there all day long to contemplate what she called, 'the great mystery of things'.

His days with Scathach turned into months and he learned not just how to throw a spear but how to become its point as it entered a man's body, cutting through skin, flesh, bone, feeling each layer as it gave way before his strength.

He learned the needle feat – tossing one hundred and fifty needles into the air, each point going into the eye of the next and falling all joined together in a circle.

He learned the apple feat – throwing three apples up and three knives and when the apples came down, they were peeled and cored.

He learned the bird feat – how to dance across the points of a hail of spears like a bird in flight.

In time Cúchulainn mastered all the ways of the warrior: the thunder feat, the swooping feat, the salmon feat of a chariot chief, the throw of the staff, the whirl of a warrior, the wheel feat, the screw feat, the blow, the quick stroke, the counterblow, the sword-edge feat, the bellow dart, the feat of the javelin, the ascent of rope, the pole throw and the leap over the poison stroke, the spurt of speed, the breath feat, the snapping mouth, the hero's scream, the wild whoop, the ardour of shout, the noise of nine, the mad roar, the stroke of precision and the stunning shot, the trussing up of a warrior, the scythe chariot and the running up a spear and righting your body on its point.

Scathach never praised him, but some days she would nod quietly to herself and on those days, he felt like the greatest warrior in the world.

Then one day, for the first time, she invited him into her seven-doored dwelling. He opened a door and a great wind rushed out and wouldn't let him in. He tried the next. It was the same. And the next and the next. From each one this great wind came. 'The food is getting cold,' she called from within.

'I am trying,' he cried.

'Remember,' she said, 'it is not where you enter, but how you enter that matters.'

Cúchulainn stepped back and bowed as if approaching the fortress of a great queen and he was inside.

She stood by the hearth staring into the fire. 'What do you see?' she asked.

'Flames,' he said.

'And behind the flames?'

'Wood,' he said.

'And behind the wood?'

'A tree,' he said.

'Become that tree,' she said.

He did.

'I burn', he said.

'Out of the fire and into the earth,' she said.

Now he stood, a tree on a mountain and she became the wind. He stiffened and she blew and broke off his unyielding branches.

'Become the mountain,' she said. He did. And she became the rain, slowly wearing him away.

'Become a stream,' she said. He did. She became the ocean waiting for him to empty himself into her, drop by drop.

'I have all the time in the world,' she said, growing more immense as he was dragged down, drowning in her depths. Finally washed ashore, he looked up to see her leaning on her hazel staff, the hearth ablaze behind her.

'Not bad,' she said. 'But you really must learn to swim.'

When they awoke the next morning, he smiled.

'Well,' she said. 'I have picked up one or two tricks in nine hundred years.'

Then there was the sound of fighting outside.

'Now,' said Scathach, 'you must face the real world.'

Aoife, a warrior woman of fierce prowess, had laid siege to the island and was holding all the other young warriors hostage.

'What she loves most are her two horses, her chariot and her charioteer,' Scathach whispered as he went.

Man to woman, they met and, as any warrior will tell you, no battle is bloodier than that.

They fought all day long until finally Aoife shattered Cúchulainn's sword and he was left holding only the hilt. Then Cúchulainn called out, 'Ah! Aoife's horses, chariot and charioteer have fallen into the river and all are washed away.' She looked round. He sprang towards her, seized her sword and now she was at his mercy.

Scathach was suddenly standing there. 'Let her live,' she said. 'She keeps me on my toes.'

'You have trained this one well,' said Aoife.

'As well as I trained you,' said Scathach. 'The two of you are well matched.'

Aoife looked at Cúchulainn and said, 'A life for a life.' And that night they slept together and she conceived a son and he gave her a golden ring for him.

'When this fits his finger,' he said, 'send him to me. No man should know his name and tell him to fight anyone who stands in his way.'

As he left, Scathach said, 'There's still lots more to learn,' and then she handed him the Gáe Bolga, the deadliest weapon in the world. 'Use it wisely.'

He returned to the gardens of the sun and yet Forgall the Wiley said he still could not have his daughter. Cúchulainn leapt over the three walls in one bound. Three times with one blow he killed nine men yet left Emer's three brothers unhurt but Forgall fled and fell from the ramparts finding his death below.

'Am I worthy now?' Cúchulainn asked.

'Yes,' said Emer as she left her father's fortress with her weight in gold.

9

THE BIRD
CATCHER

There were three great heart-throbs in Ulster: Conall the Victorious, Cuscaid the Stutterer and the Hound of Culann himself.

The women either walked with a crooked gait if they loved Conall, spoke haltingly if they loved Cuscaid, or feigned blindness if they loved Cúchulainn. For, when the Hound was angry, one of his eyes would disappear so far into his skull that not even a crane could pluck it out, while the other eye grew as big as a cauldron in which a calf could be cooked. The women of Ulster spent a lot of time bumping into each other. One day a flock of beautiful birds descended on the lake beside Emain Macha and the women began to boast of their particular hero's bird-catching prowess.

'Oh, to have a pair of those birds flying around my head like kisses in the air,' they said. 'Who could resist that?'

Reluctantly, with slingshot and net, Cúchulainn went on a bird hunt and soon returned with a pair of live birds for each of the ladies there.

The crooked walkers straightened their stance and the stutterers cleared their throats and now all the women of Ulster closed their eyes.

Cúchulainn was not interested, but returning home, he realised that he had forgotten to bring a pair of the birds back for his wife, Emer. 'Don't be angry,' he said.

'I am not angry,' she said. 'For all those women love you, yet cannot have you. And I love you and can.'

'Tomorrow I will bring you back the most beautiful birds in the world,' he said.

In the morning, Cúchulainn went back to the lake, but no birds came.

Each day he went and watched through the coming of the buds in spring, the ripening of the fruit in summer, the fall of the leaves in autumn, to the whiteness of the land in winter, when that lake became a frozen mirror to the sky. Still no bird flew equal to the beauty of his wife. Then one day, shadows darted across surface of the ice, singing filled the air and Cúchulainn looked up to see two beautiful seabirds flying side by side. He cast a stone and brought one down. Cúchulainn raced across the white and where the bird had fallen he found a naked girl lying there with blood streaming from her side. He sucked at the wound, and brought out a blood-red ruby into the cold air. She opened her eyes. 'You have saved my life,' she said. 'Now I am yours.'

'No,' he said. 'I am forbidden to lie with one whose blood I have tasted.'

She followed him back to Emain Macha. And when the women of Ulster saw her great beauty, they wondered if the man had caught the bird or if the bird had caught the man.

The winter went on and on and the warriors, faced with boredom away from battle, began to build a great structure in the snow. The form was frozen and phallic and Fergus said that in terms of himself, that was pretty much the size of it.

Then, when the men went hunting, the queen led the women to where the pillar of snow stood.

'Let us bring down this great monument,' she said. 'We will take it in turns to relieve ourselves here and the one who makes the biggest impression will be the first to eat what the men bring back tomorrow.'

'That is not what women do where I come from,' said the bird woman.

'Well then, we will not do it as women,' said the queen. 'We will do it as men, standing up.'

The pissing contest began, the queen taking precedence, followed by her ladies in order of rank. None made much headway. They asked the bird woman to try and she dissolved the snow as if spring had finally come and the edifice came tumbling down.

When they saw what she had done, they feared that this equipment would beguile their men – husbands, sons and fathers. 'We will deal with her as women,' they said, and then they fell on her like a murder of crows, clawing at her clothes, dragging her away to the ice house that stood at the edge of the lake. Inside they tore out her eyes, ripped off her ears, cut off her lips and mutilated the parts they were most afraid of.

When Cúchulainn heard the screams, he raced to the house, opened the door and saw what they had done.

Now another woman stood beside him.

'It was you that brought her down. When she fell beneath me from the sky I thought you would protect her.'

Then with her fists she set about him and with every blow she knocked him into the other world.

When they found his body, he was still breathing, but he did not open his eyes or speak a word. They carried him into the great hall at Emain Macha and laid him there.

As the weeks passed, Emer always sat by his side while his beloved Ferdiad travelled the land to try to find the cure to bring him back to life.

The months passed, and the hall became a place of pilgrimage. The sick came to touch him as if his sickness would heal their own. Some came with questions and while he moved in the other world, sometimes he still spoke in this one. Once a prince came and asked what qualities were needed to be a king. In his sickness Cúchulainn replied:

'Be humble to accept instruction from wise men.
Encourage debate in all your assemblies.
Be gracious in offering.
Be gracious in giving.

Be gracious in receiving.
Do not be a seeker of fierce and unnecessary strife.
Do not mock, deride or intimidate old men.
Do not be sluggish lest you find your death.
Do not be too hasty, lest you look ludicrous.
Do not hoard, as this will not profit you.
Do not become drunk like a flesh flea in the hall of a great king.
Listen to the historians and learn from the past.
Listen to the seers and expect the future.
Listen to the land, the living and the dead that lie beneath it.
Listen to the stories they have to tell.'

Then one day Emer could bear it no longer and she began to pound on Cúchulainn's chest, screaming for his return and he opened his eyes but he looked right through her and got up and left the hall. She followed at a distance until he came to a ring of yew trees. At its centre she could see there stood the bird woman restored. Emer watched as her husband kissed her.

'No,' cried Emer. 'I am your wife.'

Cúchulainn saw her then.

'No,' he said. 'My heart belongs to this one now, for I have been with her all this time in the other world.'

'You are in this world now,' cried Emer.

'And so is she,' said Cúchulainn, holding the bird woman close.

Emer began to sob and shake. 'All that time I sat by your side and really you were with her.'

'I cannot help myself,' he said.

She saw his nature then and knew the truth. 'I cannot make you love me. If your heart lies with her, take that love and be with her.'

At Emer's words, the bird woman rose into the sky and, looking down upon them both, said, 'She has the greater love.' With that, she flew away.

His wits left him then and he became a hound again, howling at the moon.

One day, Fergus and Ferdiad found him and they took him home, and kept him close. When spring came the bird woman sent her husband. The sea god, Manannán mac Lir, descended through the air and waved his cloak of forgetting between the two worlds.

Cúchulainn did not remember what he had lost, and yet in his dreams he saw her still.

10

SEVERED TONGUES

Every year there was a great feast where the champion's portion was served up to the boldest, the bloodiest and the best.

Warriors would bring back knickknacks of men defeated: a sword, a finger, a pair of heads. The most favoured trophy was a belt of severed tongues – it made the point and yet was practical for men always on the move.

Once Bricriu, the owner of a twisted tongue which lolled and wagged in a mouth full of bile and bitter breath, urged the Ulstermen to have the feast at a place of his construction. He had been the architect of many a man's fate and fall, knowing how to harness the power of words to wound and silences to slay. 'He will set father against son, mother against daughter,' said old King Fergus. 'Even a woman's two breasts would fight each other in his presence and the milk turn sour.'

There were always hungry-looking men at Bricriu's side, returning from sifting through the rubbish of the lives of others to drip poison into his ear. He knew all of Ulster's secrets and he looked around now into each of their eyes as if to say, 'Shall I tell them all?'

They would come on one condition; that the host would not enter his own hall.

'Agreed,' he said and he set about preparing a feast that would take days to devour, but generations to digest.

The first to arrive and be welcomed was Lóegaire, the Triumphant. Bricriu loudly sang a song of praise for him, and said, 'Inside, there is a seven-year-old boar that has been fed nothing but fresh milk and fine meal in springtime, curds and sweet milk in summer, kernels and wheat in autumn and beef broth in winter.' Then he whispered in his ear, 'I hear Conall the Victorious says he is the only warrior fit to consume it, as he has far more experience than you.'

'We'll see about that,' said Lóegaire, pushing past him to enter the hall.

'Indeed we will,' thought Bricriu. Next came Conall the Victorious himself.

'All hail to you,' cried Bricriu. 'Great champion of Ulster! Inside there is a cow who since it was a little calf has never tasted heather or twig tops, as only sweet milk, herbs, meadow hay and corn have passed its lips.'

Then he whispered in his ear, 'I hear Cúchulainn says he is the only warrior fit to consume it as you are a warrior long past his prime.'

'What?' cried Conall. 'The impudent young hound! I will show him who deserves the champion's portion.'

'I'm sure you will,' thought Bricriu.

When Cúchulainn himself came, Bricriu fell to his knees. 'Welcome great champion, beloved of all women, feared by all men. Where other warriors fail, you succeed. Inside there is the great chasm, an iron vat of beer, which has taken a hundred men a hundred days to fill with the strongest ale in Ulster.' Then he whispered in his ear, 'I hear Lóegaire and Conall say that you must not sup too much of this as you are still just a lad and can't yet hold your drink.'

'A lad!' cried Cúchulainn. 'I will show them who the man is here.'

'I bet you will,' thought Bricriu.

When the feast was laid out and beside it the tongues and other trophies, three brothers stood up.

Sedlong mac Riangabra, Lóegaire's charioteer spoke first. 'The champion's portion is rightfully my master's.'

'Not so,' said Id mac Riangabra. 'The portion belongs to my master, Conall the Victorious.'

Then Laeg mac Riangabra said, 'There is only one warrior who deserves it. My master, Cúchulainn.'

Then shields, swords and spears were seized and outside Bricriu heard the clashing of weapons as edge met edge and point met metal and he danced around in a little circle. 'Stop!' cried Conchobar. 'Let Sencha the judge decide.'

All lowered their weapons and agreed to abide by his judgment.

'Tonight,' he said, 'All three will taste the champion's portion as all are loved and seen as worthy in the eyes of the people of Ulster.'

Then the backslapping began and the men gorged and drank their fill.

'The night is young,' thought Bricriu as he saw the wives of the three heroes approaching the hall, each with fifty of their ladies.

'Welcome great queens,' he cried. 'Excellent in form, wisdom and lineage.' Then he whispered into the ear of Fedelm Fresh Heart, Lóegaire's wife. 'Tonight your husband has surpassed all the heroes of Ulster and been crowned champion of champions, and yet I hear that the other two ladies present intend to enter the hall first and take your glory as the champion's rightful consort.' Then he whispered the same into the ear of Lendabair, wife of Conall the Victorious and Emer, wife of Cúchulainn, adding, 'As the sun surpasses the stars, you outshine the women of the whole world, so do not be shamed in the sight of the warriors of Ulster. Take up your place as the Queen of the Night.'

At first, the wives led their procession of ladies slowly and gracefully in a stately and measured fashion towards the door of the hall. But as they got closer to it, their steps became shorter and quicker until finally all of the wives hitched up their skirts and started to run full pelt towards the door with their ladies in hot pursuit. Inside, as the hall shook, it sounded as if fifty chariots were thundering towards them and fearing they were under attack, the warriors seized their weapons again.

'Stay your swords,' cried Sencha. 'It is not the enemies of Ulster coming, but your angry wives whom Bricriu has set at each other's throats.'

'Our wives!' cried the three heroes. 'Shut the door lest we all be slaughtered.'

The door was bolted and the three put their backs against it. Emer reached the door first and she pushed it, but it would not open. The other two wives arrived and did likewise. 'Now we will hear not a battle of blood,' said Sencha, 'but a war of words.'

Fedelm Fresh Heart spoke first. 'I was born of a mother of freedom, sprung from loins that are royal in the beauty of peerless breeding, in the sphere of goodly demeanour. My husband, Lóegaire, triumphant over all Ulster's foemen, from enemies a defense and protection, more famous than all other heroes, in number of victories greater. So why should not his wife step first into the great feast hall?'

Then Lendabair spoke. 'Mine is a beauty of reason, with the vigour of graceful deportment. Big is his shield our defender. Majestic his gait and commanding, walking through spears of the conflict, returning with heads as his trophies which I cradle at home by the fire. My husband defends every ford from the foemen. Conall the hero of heroes! So why should not his wife enter the hall of the feast first?'

Finally Emer spoke. 'I am the standard of woman in figure, in grace and in wisdom. My husband is the mighty Cúchulainn, finely his body is fashioned, blood from his spear still spurting, wounds on his skin wide gaping. He springs into the air like a salmon, flying like a bird over water, beneath him the bloody battalions, beating down the kings in his fury. My husband rises in rage and fierceness. Open the door to the one who is first amongst women.'

Hearing this praise, Lóegaire and Conall rushed to let their wives in, but Cúchulainn lifted the whole side of the hall up so now the stars could be seen underneath and in stepped Emer first. He let the building fall and as it came crashing down, Bricriu fell on his belly into the horseshit outside. The men, now joined by the women, returned to the feast. But as the ale flowed, they began to argue again as to who was the greatest champion of all and swords were once again brandished in Bricriu's hall.

But before the fight could really take hold, there came a great hammering on the door and in crashed a strange dark creature, the shape of a man, yet three times the size. His filthy skin was covered by a rough hide and in his hands he carried a club, an axe and a block of wood.

'What is all this noise about?' he bellowed. 'I cannot sleep for all the bickering.'

'They argue over who is the greatest champion,' said Sencha.

'That is no mystery,' said the stranger. 'For there is no one here who can beat me.'

'And who are you?' asked Cúchulainn.

'I am Terror, son of Fear,' said the stranger. 'A Ballach that some call the King of the World. For I reign everywhere.'

'Big words!' said Conall the Victorious.

'From a big man,' added Lóegaire the Triumphant, looking up and up.

'Let me match them with deeds,' said the stranger. 'I challenge all those that call themselves champion to a contest. Tonight let me chop off your head and tomorrow I will return and you can chop off mine.'

The warriors laughed.

'What kind of offer is that?' they cried. 'No one would ever agree to those terms.'

'I would,' said the Ballach. 'Let me go first instead. You chop off my head now and tomorrow I will return to claim yours.' All three heroes agreed to these terms, but before anyone moved Fatneck, son of Shorthead, eager to be seen as a champion himself, stepped forward. 'Let me be the first to try,' he said. The Ballach smiled and said, 'Ah! The appetiser before the main course!' Licking his lips, he caught the eyes of the three heroes.

He put the block of wood on the ground and placed his head upon it and Fatneck took the axe, swung it high and brought it down. The head fell to the floor and the hall filled with blood.

Then the Ballach rose to his feet, picked up his head, the block, the club and the axe and made his exit from the hall, blood still streaming from his neck.

The next night when the Ballach returned, his head back on his shoulders, Fatneck was nowhere to be seen. 'No matter,' he said.

'Who will be the next to try?' Up stepped Lóegaire the Triumphant, who again took the head from the Ballach's shoulders, and the Ballach again picked it up and left the hall, returning the next night to find the warrior strangely absent. It was the same with Conall the Victorious on the next night.

'Do I detect a pattern?' asked the Ballach returning one more time. Now Cúchulainn stepped forward and he too took off the Ballach's head, and the Ballach was soon out of the door calling back, 'See you tomorrow'.

The next night, when the fierce creature returned, he found Cúchulainn waiting and without a word, the Hound took the block from the Ballach's great hands and put it on the floor and placed his head upon it. 'Stretch out your neck like a crane. Best to have a clean blow. I don't want to cause you any unnecessary suffering,' cried the Ballach. He raised the axe until it reached the ceiling and brought it crashing down. Cúchulainn, waiting for the blow to hit, felt the blunt side of the axe touch his skin, and heard 'Arise'. Cúchulainn looked up to see the Ballach was gone, and in his place, there now stood a warrior looking down at him.

'I am Cú Roí mac Dáire, the greatest champion of the other world and I say to the people of Ulster that there is only one great champion in this one.'

Then all the severed tongues began to wag and spit and cry out one name, 'Cúchulainn', and with that the terror was gone.

11

Death of a Storyteller

There were once two storytellers, Aithirne and Adnae, brothers but different in every other way. When the first one, Aithirne, was still in his mother's womb, she was refused a drink in an alehouse, but with one word from him inside, the barrels burst open and she got to quench her thirst. Adnae, the other one, was as powerful, as great a word weaver and sound shaper as his brother was a vicious versifier and wit witherer.

When Aithirne lampooned the River Mourne for not yielding him any fish, the river rose up and in a flood of anger, drowned all in its path. Adnae, seeing what his brother had done, sang a praise song and the waters drained away before him.

Once they visited Eochaidh mac Luchta, a generous one-eyed king, who offered Aithirne any gift he desired. He chose the king's remaining eye and without hesitation, the king tore it out and gave it to him. Adnae then led the blind king to the water's edge and bathed the bloody hollows. The waters turned red and when the king stood up he could see again. Both his eyes had been restored.

Then one day Aithirne went too far. After the death of Deirdre, Conchobar found a new bride, but Aithirne demanded that she sleep with him and his two sons first. She refused and Aithirne put so savage a satire upon her that it caused her body to blister and she died from the shame of it. Conchobar was furious but Cathbad warned him of the dangers of going against such a man. Cúchulainn was having none of it. He set alight Aithirne's hall and the old babbler and his two sons perished within it.

So now Adnae was the sole saga slayer of the time, dispensing wisdom in word and in deed. He had a son by the name of Neidhe, who went over the waters to be apprenticed to another master story-teller, Eochu Horsemouth. But one day, a wave brought news of his father's death and Neidhe returned to Ulster. When he arrived in Emain Macha, Bricriu of the Bitter Tongue, met him on the green.

'Hurry to your father's seat,' he said, 'for another means to take up your father's place'. Then Bricriu went to Ferchertne, Adnae's chosen successor, and said, 'Quick, for a young upstart comes to take up your rightful place.'

The two met in the stronghold of storytelling.

'Where do you come from?' asked Ferchertne.
'Not hard to tell,' said Neidhe.

> 'From the heel of a sage.
> From confluence of wisdom.
> From perfections of goodness.
> From brightness of sunrise.'

'Where do you come from?' asked Neidhe.
'Easy to say,' said Ferchertne.

> 'Along the columns of age.
> Along the land of the sun.
> Along the dwelling of the moon.
> Along the young one's navel-string.'

'How do you travel?' asked Ferchertne.
'Not hard to tell,' said Neidhe.

> 'On a king's beard.
> On a wood of age.
> On the back of a ploughing ox.
> On the light of a summer moon.'

'How do you travel?' asked Neidhe.
  'Easy to say,' said Ferchertne.

        'On the breasts of soft women.
          On the head of a spear.
         On a chariot without wheel.
         On a wheel without chariot.'

'What is your name?' asked Ferchertne.
  'Not hard to tell,' said Neidhe.

              'Fire of speech.
              Well of wealth.
            Noise of knowledge.
              Sword of song.'

'What is your name?' asked Neidhe.
  'Easy to say,' said Ferchertne.

            'Enquiry of science.
              Weft of craft.
            Casket of poetry.
          Abundance of ocean.'

'What art do you practise?' asked Ferchertne.
  'Not hard to tell,' said Neidhe.

              'Piercing flesh.
        Tossing away shamelessness.
            Defusing knowledge.
            Stripping speech.'

'What art do you practise?' asked Neidhe.
  'Easy to say,' said Ferchertne.

'Fury of inspiration.
Structure of mind.
Clear arrangement.
A celebrated road.'

'Who is your father?' asked Ferchertne.
'Not hard to tell,' said Neidhe

'I am poetry, son of scrutiny.
Scrutiny, son of meditation.
Meditation, son of lore.
Lore, son of enquiry.
Enquiry, son of investigation.
Investigation, son of great knowledge.
Great knowledge, son of great sense.
Great sense, son of understanding.
Understanding, son of wisdom.'

'Who is your father?' asked Neidhe.
'Easy to say,' said Ferchertne.

'I am the son of the man not yet born.
I am the son of the first utterance of every living thing.
I am the son of the cry of the dead.
I am the son of the question that you ask at first light.
I am the son of the thought that you have at midday.
I am the son of the answer that you give in your sleep.'

'Then you are my father,' said Neidhe, kneeling before him.
'And you are my son,' said Ferchertne. 'The one to follow me when I am gone. Sit beside me now, and I will tell you the story of my death.

'Once there was a wild shape shifter named Cú Roí mac Dáire who was known as the king of the world.

'One day he and Cúchulainn ventured into the other world and brought back three cows, a cauldron of plenty and a beautiful woman named Blathnat. When Cúchulainn would not share the spoils, Cú Roí thrust him into the earth up to his armpits, cut off his hair and rubbed cow dung into his head.

'Cú Roí gathered up the cows, threw Blathnat over his shoulder and carried off the cauldron.

'Cúchulainn avoided the Ulstermen for a whole year after that until his hair had grown back.

'On his return, they held a great feast for him with pigs roasting and a hundred vats of every kind of ale. When the moon was high in the sky, Cúchulainn cried, "Let's finish this at my place!"

'Then Laeg, who possessed the three virtues of charioteering – turning around, straight backing, leap over gap – brought Cúchulainn's horses to a furious sudden start. All jumped into their chariots and chased after them.

'They raced through the green of Dun-da-Benn to Cathar Osrin, to Dun-Rigain, to Dlarli and by the shores of Olarli into Mag Maca, into Sliab Fúait, and into Ath an Foriare, to Port Not of Cúchulainn, into Mag Muirthene, into Crich Saithi, across the stream of the Boyne, into Mag Breg and Meath, into May Lena, into Cliather Cell, across the Bronas of Blacha then left towards the gap of Mer, daughter of Treg, then right to the hills of Eblinne, daughter of Guaire, across the fair stream which is called the river of Ua Cathbed.

'Every hill they came to, they flattened. Every wood they passed through, they cleared. Every river they crossed, they emptied and left dry, all the while, showing their bare backsides to startled deer and singing songs of their battles both in and out of bed.

'On they went into the great plain of Munster, through the middle of Artine and into Sertinia, then right towards the rocks of Loch Gair across the pool of Marig to Cliu Mail maic Ugaine, into the territory of Deise Beg and then into an unknown land.

'Ahead of them, two old seers, Crom Deroil and Crom Derail were watching. "A great storm is coming," said Crom Deroil.

'"The sky is clear," said Crom Derail.

'"The storm is on the ground in the shape of men," said Crom Deroil.

"'That is just the yew trees you see, swaying in the wind," said Crom Derail.

"'Those trees you see are carrying spears and swords," said Crom Deroil.

"'Those spears and swords you see are the antlers of the stags and the tusks of the boars of the forest."

"'Those stags and boars you see are riding on horses."

"'Those horses you see are the flocks of the sheep and the herds of the cattle let out to pasture."

'Their master, Cú Roí mac Dáire, called for silence.

'As the sun rose over the earth, all three could now see the warriors of Ulster fast approaching. Cú Roí welcomed them into his fortress. Within there stood a house of wood, a house of stone and a house of iron.

'He asked them in which one they wished to spend the night. They all spoke at once, disagreeing, until Sencha the judge said, "Let Cúchulainn decide."

"'The house of iron," he said.

"'The worst possible choice," muttered Bricriu under his breath.

'As they slept in their stocious sleep, having their fall down dreams, outside, the houses of wood and stone were torn down and the wood piled high around the house of iron and the stones pushed against the doors. Cú Roí set all ablaze. 'I smell breakfast cooking,' said Cúchulainn.

"'That's not breakfast. That's us," said Bricriu.

'Suddenly all sobered up at once and when they broke through the doors, they found Cú Roí waiting there. "It was a cold night," he said. "I didn't want you to catch your death." He offered them shelter in his own house for the rest of the night. They preferred to sleep in the open under the stars with some of their own men standing guard.

'In the morning Cú Roí appeared with a most beautiful woman. "You know my wife," he said to Cúchulainn. It was Blathnot. She looked at her husband and then at the champion of Ulster and thought she had not got the better part of the deal. When he looked at her he could only think of the time he had cow dung rubbed into his head.

'Later in secret, she came to him. "Take me away from this dark place," she said, "and I will be yours."

'"Cú Roí is one creature I cannot kill," said Cúchulainn.

'"Not without my help," she said. "He is invulnerable, because he does not keep his soul in his body like other men."

'"Where then?" asked Cúchulainn.

'"Promise to take me," she said. He promised.

'"His soul resides in a golden salmon in a dark pool," she said. "It can only be destroyed with his own sword." A plan was hatched there and then.

'She went to Cú Roí, placed her arms around him and began lousing his head, bathed him and then bound his hair to the bedpost.

'He closed his eyes and smiled in anticipation of what would happen next.

'She took his sword and dropped it out of the window into the river that flowed past the fortress and the rushing waters carried it down to the pool where Cúchulainn was waiting.

'There swam the golden salmon. Cúchulainn picked up the sword. Cú Roí opened his eyes and as Cúchulainn thrust the sword into its heart, the last thing that Cú Roí ever saw was his wife smiling back at him.

'Cúchulainn made his way back up the valley, but just as he reached the fortress, I, Ferchertne, the storyteller to the king of the world, saw what she had done. I rushed towards Blathnot, grabbed her in my arms and, embracing her, threw myself out of the window. We both fell to our deaths on the rocks below.'

Ferchertne was gone and Neidhe took up his father's place in the stronghold of the story.

12

The
Homecoming

As the sun rose over the sea, a golden boy in a boat of bronze rowed towards the shores of Ulster. With slingshot and stone, the lad stunned the seabirds flying overhead. Catching them as they fell, reviving and releasing them once more into the air. Soon the sky was full of dark dots, the sound of beating wings and breaking waves, a whole world eager to be knocked unconscious and brought back to life again.

High on the cliff tops, Leborcham, the king's messenger was watching and she sent word to him of what she had seen and heard. It was a grave Conchobar who gathered his warriors around him that morning. 'They say he is no more than seven. If he can do all they say, then what would his father, his uncles, be capable of? Surely they would grind us into dust! The boy must not be allowed to land,' commanded the king. 'Condere! Find out who he is and where he is from. But do not let him step ashore.'

'Why Condere and not I?' each man grumbled in turn, like boys who had not been picked first for the team.

'That is not hard to tell,' said the king. 'Only Condere has the reason and the eloquence for the task.'

So off he set reaching the sea just as the lad's little boat reached the shore. 'You must go back,' said Condere. 'There's nothing for you here.'

'That is not what my mother says,' said the boy.

'And who might she be?' asked Condere.

'That I cannot say,' replied the boy.

'Then your name, pleasant lad?' asked Condere.

'That I cannot say,' replied the boy.

'Then tell me of the land where you are from,' said Condere.

'That I ...'

'Cannot say,' finished Condere. 'Then speak of what you can say.'

'I can say,' said the boy, 'that I will fight any man who stands in my way.'

'Will you fight Cethern of the bloodied blade, Conall Cernach the boar swallower, Amairgin the poet, Sencha MacAilella the peacemaker or indeed the king himself?'

'I will fight each in turn or all together,' said the boy, 'if they come to greet me on this shore.'

'And in the killing will you find what you are looking for?' asked Condere.

'You have come armed with words when I seek action,' said the warlike child.

'Well, I will not fight a foe,' said Condere, 'who does not yet reach the buckle at my belt.' And he turned and went back to the king.

'That hairless youth brings shame upon us all,' cried Conall the Victorious. 'Let me go and I'll drag out his whole story from first to last.'

The king agreed and Conall reached the sea just as the boy stepped ashore. 'That's far enough,' he said. 'Now, tell me your name and there'll be no more trouble.'

'That I cannot say,' said the boy.

'Then let me help you with your tongue,' said Conall advancing towards him. The lad put a stone in his sling and sent it whistling, felling Conall in one blow. And before he knew it, the boy had trussed him up tight with the strap of his own shield.

'Send someone else!' cried Conall the Victorious. Cúchulainn could take no more.

'I will find out who this boy is, and where he is from and send him back there,' said Cúchulainn. Emer held him back.

'Do not go to the water's edge,' she said. 'He is just a child.'

'And to be beaten by a child would not be the greatest shame of all?' asked Cúchulainn, reaching for his spear.

'But what if that child was yours?' asked Emer, clutching Cúchulainn's cloak.

'That is a woman's question,' said Cúchulainn. 'Men must defend what is theirs against the world. Today the world comes as a boy. Tomorrow the boy returns a man with a thousand others to destroy us all.'

'But what if that boy is the one who resembles his father most?' asked Emer.

'Then let the blood that passed through his father's veins be spilt by my hand and flow into the land for the honour of Ulster.'

'A bull that kills his own calf murders his own future,' said Emer. But it was too late, Cúchulainn was already gone.

As Cúchulainn reached the sea, the boy on the shore was now silhouetted against a dying sun. The figure in that shimmering furnace seemed to flicker and change from boy to man then into a great god formed out of fire and light.

'At last an opponent worthy of me,' said Cúchulainn.

'We are indeed well matched,' said the boy.

'I have heard of your games,' said Cúchulainn.

'Would you rather hear the story or play a part?' asked the boy.

'I am never an idle spectator,' said Cúchulainn.

'Good,' said the boy. 'I am tired of playing alone.'

'What is your name?' asked Cúchulainn.

'That I cannot say,' said the boy.

'Then speak to me with fists for my patience is at an end,' said Cúchulainn.'

'Let us bring matters to a head then,' said the boy. And with one swift skillful stroke of his sword, he cut off Cúchulainn's hair leaving him as bald as a baby. Now the great frenzy was upon Cúchulainn. He lunged at the boy and the two of them fell fighting beneath the waves. Each tried to drown the other until exhausted Cúchulainn let loose the Gáe Bolga, the lightning spear, which tore into the boy's body through skin, flesh and bone. 'Now that is something Scathach never taught me,' said the boy, growing pale.

'Who are you?' asked Cúchulainn.

The boy reached up to touch Cúchulainn's face and it was only then that Cúchulainn noticed the curving glint of sun light upon his thumb. It was a golden ring.

'When this ring fits his finger, send him to me. Let no man know his name and tell him to fight anyone who stands in his way.'

He carried the boy to where the warriors of Ulster were waiting. 'If only I could have grown as tall as you,' said the boy. I would have been the greatest of you all and we could have ruled the world.'

Then each warrior in turn embraced him and the last breath left his body. Cúchulainn lifted up the boy who was now light in his arms. 'This is my son, Conlla, who I have slain for the honour of Ulster.'

For three days and three nights, no calf was allowed to suckle and the bellowed grief of their mothers filled the land.

All the while Cúchulainn stood on the shore fighting the waves, trying to turn back the tide.

13

CROW AND CROWN

Two hanged men are made to dance in the daylight, but when the darkness comes, no one dares go near. It is Samhain, the time when all the worlds meet and men believe the dead walk the earth.

In the royal hall at Connacht, the pigs were being turned and following the roasting and toasting came the boasting of brave deeds done. Queen Medb with King Ailill beside her stood up and rattled her charms.

'As you are all so brave, I'm sure one of you wouldn't mind tying this withe of willow around the ankle of one of those corpses hanging out there.'

Now all who had spoken were silent and studying the stone floor as if it was studded with stars.

'None of you?' she laughed. 'Not even for your queen?' No one stirred. 'I suppose,' she said with a smile, 'it's better to play dead than meet the dead on a night like this.'

'I will go,' said a young lad now standing before the queen.

'What's your name?'

'Nerai, ma'am.'

She handed him the withe, saying, 'Better a brave boy than a scared man for a task like this.'

It was a cold crisp evening. The gallows creaked as Nerai approached the hanged men and he could see a crow perched silently between them. The wind blew and one of the corpses seemed to turn to meet him. He reached up and tied the withe around its stiff ankle, but the withe slipped off and fell to the ground. He tied it again. It fell again. A third time he tied it and a third time it fell. 'Let me give you a hand,' said the corpse and, lifting his leg, he tied it tightly around his own ankle.

'Thank you very much,' said Nerai.

'Not at all,' said the corpse. 'Now will you help me?'

'I'll do my best,' said Nerai.

'This rope around my neck has given me a great thirst and I would like a drink.'

'What about your friend?' asked Nerai.

'He's no friend of mine,' said the corpse. 'He lied to save his own skin, but instead we both got strung up here together.' So Nerai cut him down and carrying him on his back, went off to find some refreshment.

First they came to a house standing in a ring of fire. 'There will be no drink for us here,' said the corpse and they travelled on until they came to a house surrounded by a ring of water.

'There will be no drink for us here either,' said the corpse and they travelled on until they came to an ordinary looking house.

'This will do nicely,' said the corpse.

Inside there was drink aplenty, and after the corpse had guzzled it down, he spat the last few drops into the faces of the people who slept there and they all stopped breathing.

'What did you do that for?' asked Nerai.

'This is the other hanged man's family,' smiled the corpse. 'I thought they would be missing him.'

'I think it's time we went back now,' said Nerai.

But when they returned to the gallows, they found the great hall of Connacht had become a blackened, charred ruin and the heads of the king and queen stuck on wooden spikes in front of it.

'Who has done this?' asked Nerai.

'Let us find out,' said the corpse. And as the hanged man whispered in his ear, Nerai walked from this world into the next.

Back in Ulster, Cúchulainn was waking to the sound of a bull bellowing. It was still dark. He jumped out of bed and soon met his charioteer on the road. 'Did you hear it?' he asked.

'Aye,' said Laeg.

'From which direction?'

'From the north-west, across the great highway leading to Caill Cuan.'

'Wait here until I find out what this means,' said Cúchulainn.

He had not travelled long when he saw a strange sight coming towards him. A one-legged horse was pulling a chariot, its pole passing through the body of the beast, the point piercing the halter on its head. Within the chariot, there sat a fierce-looking woman of middle years, with a cloak of raven feathers around her shoulders and a crown of crow claws upon her head. Beside the chariot there walked a giant of a man driving a cow before him, a staff of hazelwood in his hand.

'What business do you have with that cow?' asked Cúchulainn.

'What business is it of yours?' asked the woman.

'I was speaking to the man,' said Cúchulainn.

'The cow and the man are mine,' said the woman, 'and I asked what business is it of yours?'

'All the cattle in Ulster are my business,' said Cúchulainn.

'This cow is not from these parts,' said the woman.

'Do you have any proof?' asked Cúchulainn.

'Would you take a story as proof?' asked the woman.

'If it were true,' said Cúchulainn.

'When is a story not true?' asked the woman.

'Tell your tale then,' said Cúchulainn.

'In the other world there is a well. Every day a blind man with a lame man on his back goes to the well. "Is it there?" asks the blind man. The lame man leans over and looks in. "It is indeed," he answers. "Then let us go away again," says the blind man.'

'Is what there?' asked Cúchulainn.

'The crown of the king of the world,' said the woman. 'The blind man and the lame man are its guardians, for the king knows that neither can steal it without the assistance of the other and while one might betray him, he doesn't believe both would.'

'And what is this crown like?' asked Cúchulainn.

'It is like a ring of stars fallen from the sky,' said the woman. 'And a man from this world, by the name of Nerai, carrying a corpse upon his back, once looked into the well and his eyes were soon on fire. But there was a woman at the well, even more beautiful than the crown and she took Nerai's hand and soon there was a baby coming. Then one day as Nerai tended that woman's herd, he fell fast asleep, and I took the cow that is before you now.'

'So you are a thief,' said Cúchulainn.

'I am a gift giver,' said the woman in the chariot. 'I am returning the cow to its owner. When I took her she was empty. Now she carries a wondrous child from the great brown bull of Ulster; this bull calf will burst out of her and bring havoc into your world.'

'Who are you?' asked Cúchulainn.

'My name is Faebor-beg-beoil cuimdiuir folt sceb-gairit sceo uath and my companion is called Uar-gaeth-seo Luachar-sceo.'

Now even in those days, such names were ridiculous and Cúchulainn leapt into the chariot and placed the point of his spear at the parting of her hair.

'Who are you?' asked Cúchulainn again.

'I am a female satirist. The one who speaks the lies that tell the truth; she who has the wit to wail and wonder at the world. I am also a lady under your protection and in need of a little space.'

Cúchulainn jumped down from the chariot. 'Who are you?' he asked again.

'I am just a little short of a crown,' she answered.

'No more riddles,' said Cúchulainn. And with that, the cow, the man and the chariot disappeared and the woman was now a crow watching from a tree.

'What are you?' cried Cúchulainn.

'I am she they call the Great One, the mighty Crow Queen. I am the Morrigu.'

'If I had known who you were, I would have destroyed you when I had the chance,' said Cúchulainn.

'Timing is everything,' said the satirist perched on the branch. 'When my bull calf brings about the end of everything, I will be the bird watching over your death.'

Back in the other world Nerai was waking to the sound of a bull calf being born into the world. This was a bit of a surprise as the cow hadn't seemed to be pregnant when he had gone to sleep. When he returned home with the herd, his wife said, 'It is time for you to go back to your own people and warn them of what is to come.'

'But my people are all dead and the royal hall destroyed,' he said.

'What you saw, my love, was the future. Tonight is Samhain when the gap between the worlds can be crossed and when the warriors of this world will attack yours. Go and warn your people.'

'But who will believe me?' asked Nerai.

'Here,' said his wife. 'Take the fruits of summer with you as proof.'

She handed him wild garlic, primrose and golden fern. 'Hurry now,' she said.

He left his wife and child then, and made his way back to his own world. There still stood the royal hall of Connacht as strong and as impenetrable as it had always been. He stepped back inside and there was everyone as before, laughing, drinking and making merry.

'That was quick, lad,' said the king and all the others cheered.

He told his tale and they laughed even more. Then he showed them the gifts his wife had given him. 'None of these could have been picked now in this world,' said Queen Medb. She ordered her warriors to lay waste the other king's realm and bring back his crown and that bull calf.

Now they were no longer scared of the dark. This was war.

When the bull calf was brought out into this world, it grew to be mighty like its father and it raced across the plain of Cruachan and there met the mighty white bull of Connacht, the Finnbennach. They fought day and night until finally the Finnbennach defeated the young bull from the other world. It bellowed three times before it died.

'What did he say?' Queen Medb asked her cowherd.

'He bellowed that his father will avenge his death.'

'And who is his father?'

'His father is the Donn Cuailnge, the great brown bull of Ulster.'

'Now that is one battle I would like to see,' said Queen Medb, placing the crown of the other world upon her head.

14

Husbands
and Wives

In the beginning, the bridal bed is usually busy, but over time it becomes another kind of battlefield. This is as true for kings and queens as it is for you and me.

That night, as they lay together, Queen Medb and King Ailill were engaged in a little pillow talk. 'You were a lucky woman to get myself and all I possessed,' said Ailill.

'Lucky?' replied Medb. 'Was I not the High King's daughter?'

'You were,' he said.

'And did not my father give me this whole province to rule?' she asked.

'He did,' he said.

'And did I not come with thirty thousand warriors who were just my own bodyguard?' she asked.

'You did,' he said.

'And did I not have the pick of all the kings in Ireland?' she asked.

'You did,' he said.

'And did I not leave the greatest of those, my husband Conchobar, for you?'

'You did,' he said.

'And did you not come seeking me?'

'I did for sure,' said Ailill. 'For you were the most beautiful, the bravest and the cleverest of his daughters.'

'Were?' she said.

'Are,' he said. 'Even though you claimed the queerest sort of bride price.'

'All I asked for was a man who was my equal in all things,' said Medb with a smile. 'A man without meanness, without jealousy and without fear, for I am the most generous of women and no other has taken so many lovers nor killed so many men. I needed a husband who understood my ways because they were also his.'

'And we have been well matched ever since,' said Ailill. 'Equal in all things.'

'Not all,' said the queen. They argued until the sun came up and in the morning, Ailill ordered that everything each of them possessed be brought so they could be judged and seen by all.

First were brought the wooden spoons, bowls and basins, the iron vats, cups and tubs.

They possessed the same.

Then the thumb rings, bracelets, chains and cloths of gold.

All could see that they were equal.

Then their flocks of sheep were gathered.

Both had the same amount and quality of wool. Each had a splendid ram that were twins in nature and ability to bring the ewes to lamb.

Then the swine were brought and each pig was as fat as the other, and each boar as fierce and finely tusked.

Then there came the horses and the steeds.

Each had a stallion, which was well proportioned.

Then their two great herds of cattle were rounded up and reckoned.

Each herd was equal in number and the fullness of their udders.

Then the bulls were brought and counted and counted, again and again.

The queen had one less.

This was not just about numbers. Before them now stood the mightiest beast in their realm – the Finnbennach, the white bull of Connacht, Ailill's pride and joy. The queen looked at her husband as if to say, 'so where is my bull?' In truth the Finnbennach was hers, or had been. Born from one of her cows, the bull deemed himself too worthy to be owned by a woman and had taken his place amongst the king's cattle.

Since that day, although she was the greatest of queens, she felt, in the eyes of the world, like the poorest of women. If she could not possess him, well, then no one else would.

'There is none like him,' said Ailill.

'I know of another,' said the Queen.

'Where?'

'In the field of Daire mac Fincha, in the province of Ulster there stands his equal, the Donn Cuailage, the great brown bull of Ulster.'

'Then my love,' said the king, 'to prove I am still your equal in all things, I will get him for you.'

So messengers were sent with the offer of fifty heifers, a gift of land equal to his own and, for good measure, Medb threw herself into the bargain as well. All for the loan of the bull for just one year.

When Daire mac Finch heard the terms, it was Medb's giving of herself that sealed the deal. But that night drink loosened the tongues of the messengers and one was overheard to say, 'it is well for him that he agreed our terms, for if he had not, we would have taken the bull anyway.' The others laughed.

The next morning, the deal was off and the messengers kicked out without even a dried up old cow, never mind a mighty bull.

The frightened messengers returned with the news to their queen.

'No matter,' she said. 'All that is changed is that he will not be getting the bull back. Now it is not his for the giving, but ours for the taking.'

15

WAR
CRIES

The Queen and King of Connacht, gathered the tribes of the four provinces into a great army on the borderlands of Ulster. Now under attack, the Ulstermen were under Macha's curse, writhing on the ground, suffering the birth pangs. Medb made a circuit of the camp and inspected all the troops assembled there. Returning to her husband, she said, 'The Galeoin troop of three thousand from Leinster cannot come with us.'

'What is wrong with them?' asked Ailill.

'Nothing,' said Medb. 'That is the problem. While the others were still making space for their camp, they had already pitched theirs and were eating their fill. While the others ate, the Galeoin harpers played as they slept.'

'They sound like fine warriors,' said Ailill.

'Too fine,' said Medb. 'If they come, then they will get all the glory for our victory.'

'Then let them stay,' said Ailill.

'No, they cannot stay,' said Medb.

'Why not?' asked Ailill.

'When we are away they may seize our lands,' said Medb.

'Well if they can neither come nor stay,' said Ailill, 'what are we going to do with them?'

'Kill them,' said Medb.

'Kill them!' repeated Ailill.

'Yes,' said Medb, 'and the sooner the better.'

'No,' said Fergus, striding into the tent. 'If you turn against the Galeoin men, then my company of warriors and the three thousand troop of each of the seven kings of Munster will turn against you.'

'Then what is the solution to the problem?' asked Medb.

'We will tell the Galeoin men that their strength and prowess is lacking in the other troops gathered and scatter them across the army,' said Fergus.

'A sound plan,' said a relieved Ailill, who often realised when the queen had gone too far without knowing how to stop her going any further.

This was done and the army advanced with Fergus at its head, leading them on a great detour south to give time for the Ulster men, who were his kin, to recover from their labour pains. When Medb challenged the route he was taking, Fergus said, 'Never underestimate the element of surprise.' When he could fool her no longer, they headed north into the great forest south of Fid Duin.

At the heart of the forest, Cúchulainn lay with the prophetess, Fedelm. He got up and sniffed the air. 'Yes. They are coming,' she said. 'Time to return to your charioteer.'

Not long after, Medb found her waiting there.

'What are you doing in the woods?' asked Medb.

'The forest shields me from the future,' said Fedelm.

'You have the sight?' asked Medb.

'I do,' said Fedelm.

'What do you see, then?'

'I see crimson. I see red,' said Fedelm.

'On whose men are those colours splattered?'

'I cannot see clearly through the trees.'

'Then we will have to cut them down.'

The forest was razed to the ground and that place has been known as Slechta, 'the Cut', ever since.

'Now what do you see?' asked Medb.

'I see crimson. I see red,' said Fedelm.

'Yes,' said Medb. 'But what else do you see?'

'I see a forge hound snarling at the ground. I see a distorted man, ripping and roaring across the earth.'

'Do you see crimson? Do you see red?' asked Medb.

'Yes,' said Fedelm. 'He is covered in crimson and red.'

'Yes!' cried Medb.

'Bathed in blood,' said Fedelm.

'Yes!' cried Medb again.

'Bathed in the blood of all the warriors he has slain,' said Fedelm.

'Oh,' said Medb.

'I see crimson. I see red,' said Fedelm, 'as the heads of your warriors rain down like the acorns in the forest you destroyed, a shower of slaughter. Now a great warrior queen wears a cloak of crimson and red.'

'This girl just sees for the other side,' said Medb, but even she could not help being a little unnerved by the encounter.

Deeper in the forest, Cúchulainn, with one stroke of his sword, cut a tree into the shape of a four-fingered fork, and placed it standing up in a stream. Err and Innel were riding ahead of the army, with their two charioteers. When they reached the stream, Cúchulainn cut off their heads, and stuck one on each prong of the tree fork.

When the rest of the army arrived they saw their comrades heads, four pairs of eyes wide open, staring back at them.

Medb wondered what all this meant. 'It means,' said Fergus, 'that Cúchulainn is awake.'

'Why is he not with the other Ulstermen on their bellies in awe of a woman's suffering?' asked Medb.

'Because he is not a man,' said Fergus. 'While the curse falls on them like a bitter blow, it comes to him like the tender cooings of a doting aunt.'

They rode on until their path was blocked by a fallen oak. Along the trunk, Cúchulainn had carved 'No one can pass until a warrior jumps over this in his chariot.'

Medb's men took up the challenge and thirty chariots were broken before Fergus succeeded.

Orlan, the queen's son, rode out with his charioteer to find wood to repair the broken chariots. He found a tree and pointing it out to his man, he went further into the forest to relieve himself. The charioteer cut the tree, stripped off the bark and rubbed it smooth. All the while Cúchulainn watched from the branches of another tree. Then, landing lightly behind the charioteer he asked, 'What are you doing friend?'

The charioteer turned with a start, but seeing a friendly face, said, 'Making chariot shafts. That wild bastard Cúchulainn has caused us to break our own.'

'Really! What a shame!' said Cúchulainn. 'Can I help?'

'I'd be grateful,' said the charioteer. 'Do you want to cut down the trunks or take off the branches?'

'I'll take off the branches,' said Cúchulainn and with one swift movement, the trunks were smooth.

'You've done this before,' said the charioteer.

'No. This is my first time,' said Cúchulainn.

'Well, you've certainly got the knack to it,' said the charioteer. 'Who are you?'

'My name is Cúchulainn,' said Cúchulainn.

'Oh,' said the charioteer, now beginning to edge away from him.

'Do not be afraid,' said Cúchulainn. 'I'm very fond of charioteers. It's their masters I have trouble with.'

Then Orlan returned and Cúchulainn took off his head and then tied it to the charioteer's back, saying, 'Do not relieve yourself of this burden until you are inside the queen's camp or else I will take your head off too.'

When Medb saw the charioteer coming, she rushed out of the camp and took the head of her son off the man's back and cradled it in her arms. 'He warned me,' said the charioteer, 'if I didn't carry it on my back into the camp, then he would take off my ...' A stone hummed through the air and the charioteer's head left his shoulders.

Cúchulainn was very fond of charioteers but only if they did exactly what he said.

Away from all the commotion, the brown bull was grazing peacefully until a dark shadow descended and the Crow Queen settled in the shape of a bird on his back.

'Great one! They are coming. Those who seek to tether you – to chain you to a post so that you can no longer roam across the land. Then you will be slave to their desires.' The brown bull kept on chomping the grass.

'There were once two crows,' continued the Crow Queen, 'a mother and her son,' and the mother said, "Listen to me. If you ever see a man stooping, be on your guard for he may be picking up a stone to throw at you." At that very moment, a man did come. But he did not stoop, for the stone was in his pocket and soon the mother crow was dead at his feet. "It is a better lesson taught by the man than the mother," sang the little crow as he flew away.' The brown bull raised his head and with his fifty heifers followed the dark one to safer pastures.

16

The Wooden Sword

It was said that it was only Fergus, the old king, who could satisfy the queen's great appetite. One day, Ailill sent a servant to spy on the two of them. He found them lying together and, unseen, the man took Fergus's sword from its sheath and returned to show it to Ailill. 'Hide it,' said the king.

When Fergus awoke he found his sword gone and as Medb slept, he slipped away into the forest and fashioned himself a new sword made of wood.

That place has been known as Fid Mor Thruaille, Big Scabbard Wood, ever since.

The next time Ailill saw Fergus, Medb's husband could not stop laughing.

'Has she blunted your real sword?' he asked.

'I thought you would be angry,' said Fergus.

'No,' said Ailill. 'She would sleep with every warrior here if she thought it would bring us victory and I love her all the more for it.'

'Thank the gods then,' said Fergus, 'that at least my mighty spear is still intact.'

They were still laughing when Medb walked into the tent. 'What's so funny?' she asked.

'Oh, nothing my dear,' said Ailill. 'Just men's talk'.

But there was little laughter to be had in the coming weeks and months as Cúchulainn picked off Connacht men one by one and three by three and sometimes ten by ten and the warriors became so fearful that they would even go in groups of thirty just to take a leak at the edge of the camp.

It was decided to send Fergus to the ford to try and make peace with the ferocious Hound.

Reluctantly he allowed Etarcamal, Medb's foster son, to go with him. But knowing he was an arrogant young pup, he made him promise that he would not insult or rile Cúchulainn in any way.

'I see two chariots coming,' said Laeg. 'In one there sits an unknown warrior. In the other, your foster father.'

Cúchulainn embraced Fergus warmly and then stepping back, smiled and said, 'I hear you made wood with the queen and now you have to carry a stick in your scabbard.'

'I'll stick something in your scabbard, my lad, if you're not careful,' said Fergus. 'Now, let's get down to business.'

Cúchulainn proposed that instead of random slaughter, each day he would meet one of their warriors at the ford and face them in single combat. When Fergus turned to take these terms back to Queen Medb, Etarcamal just looked at Cúchulainn. 'What are you staring at?' asked Cúchulainn.

'You,' said Etarcamal.

'What do you see?' asked Cúchulainn.

'A myth, which close up, looks just like a man. No! A boy who perhaps should be playing with a wooden sword himself.'

'As you are under Fergus's protection,' said Cúchulainn. 'I will let that pass.'

'Then tomorrow, I will be the first to face you at the ford,' said Etarcamal.

'You will not be the last,' said Cúchulainn.

As Etarcamal rode off behind Fergus, he suddenly ordered his charioteer to turn back again. 'Back so soon?' said Cúchulainn.

'I cannot wait till tomorrow,' said Etarcamal.

Cúchulainn cut the ground from beneath his feet. 'Go home. You are still under Fergus's protection.'

'I want that big head of yours,' said Etarcamal.

'Have this instead,' said Cúchulainn as with his sword he cut away Etarcamal's clothes leaving him standing there naked without a cut upon his skin. 'Now go home,' said Cúchulainn.

'No,' said Etarcamal raising his sword as Cúchulainn brought his own down through the crown of Etarcamal's head, splitting him to his naval.

When Fergus returned to see Etarcamal's body on the ground, he flew at Cúchulainn in a rage. 'You have dishonoured me. He was under my protection.' But Cúchulainn returned not one blow.

When Etarcamal's charioteer told what had happened, Fergus pierced Etarcamal's heels and dragged his body behind the chariot back to the camp.

'Harsh treatment for my foster son,' said Medb.

'He was arrogant,' said Fergus.

'Ah well then,' she said. 'He has learned a worthy lesson, which should be valuable to him in the next world.'

Then Fergus explained Cúchulainn's terms. Ailill said, 'Better to lose one man every day than a hundred every night.' Word was sent to Cúchulainn that his conditions were accepted.

The next morning, Nadcramtail, taking nine charred darts with him, was the first to face Cúchulainn who was busy bird catching. Nadcramtail threw one dart after another at him and Cúchulainn danced on the point of each, as if he himself was a bird in flight. Nadcramtail was soon dead upon the ground.

The morning after that, the brute, Curmac Dalth stood there. Cúchulainn dispatched him with an apple he had been juggling absentmindedly. Lath mac Dabro came the next and then Cur mac Dalath, then Lath mac Dabro and Foric mac trin-aignech, then Srubgaile. One by one all were slain and this is how the land was first named.

> Cer died on the meadow named after him.
> Fota in the field now called by his name.
> Bomailce on the ford named after him.
> Salach in the marsh called by his name.
> Muinne on his hill.

Luair in Lethbera Luair
Fertoithle in Toithli.

The places called, ever after, for the men who had fallen there.

Then Fergus was sent again to face his foster son.

'I see you are back with your wooden sword,' said Cúchulainn.

'If it was an iron one, yet still I would not harm you,' said Fergus.

'Then what do you ask of me?'

'To yield today and on another day, I will yield to you,' said Fergus.

Cúchulainn agreed and both men left the ford alive.

The next day, Medb sent Cailitin with his twenty-eight sons to face the Hound, saying that as they all were of one flesh and blood, they counted as one opponent. For good measure, all their weapons were dipped in poison.

One of the Ulster exiles, Fiachra mac Fir Febe was sent by Fergus to follow them. When they found him, Cúchulainn was bathing at the ford. They let loose all their spears together. Cúchulainn did the rim feat, all twenty-nine spears embedding themselves in his shield.

Then they came at him with their swords and Cúchulainn yelled 'Unfair fight!' and Fiachra leapt from his chariot and cut off all twenty-nine hands raised against the Hound. Fighting side by side, they finished them off.

That night, by the water's edge, Cúchulainn raised twenty-nine standing stones for the Cailitin and his sons.

17

FOUR DEATHS AND NO WEDDING

The next day, a beguiling girl on the back of a white red-eared cow rode towards the ford. A hundred head of cattle followed in her wake.

'I come as a bride with my own dowry,' said the girl.

'She is indeed a mighty beast,' said Cúchulainn.

'Yes,' said the girl. 'One milking quenches the thirst of a thousand warriors. Once a woman stole her from me, but as she milked, she was washed away in the flow and drowned in the white lake she had made.'

'A dangerous creature then,' said Cúchulainn.

'Not if you know how to handle her,' said the girl, smiling.

'But I have a wife already,' said Cúchulainn.

'In this world, yes,' said the girl. 'But what of the next?'

'The next world can wait for now,' said Cúchulainn. 'I am at my work, and have no time for the distraction of a girl's backside.'

'Well, I came with a blessing and now I leave with a curse,' said the girl. 'The next time we meet, I will hinder you and offer you many a distraction.'

'A young girl like you?' said Cúchulainn.

'I will become this cow and run you into the ground,' cried the girl, now struggling to hold her shape.

'I will break your leg and bring you down,' said Cúchulainn.

'Then I will turn into an eel and pull you under the water,' hissed the girl.

'I will crush you,' said Cúchulainn.

'Then I will change into a wolf', screeched the girl.

'I will tear out your throat,' said Cúchulainn, 'and none but my blessing will heal you, and that I will never give.' With those words, the Crow Queen and her herd were gone.

In her tent, Medb sat beside her daughter, Finnabair, when in came Ailill with Fer Baeth mac Fir Bend. 'She's yours,' said the queen, 'if you are man enough to face the Hound tomorrow. For if you have the courage to do that, then you may indeed be brave enough to be my son-in-law.'

Between each mouthful of wine gulped down, the girl pressed her lips to his, and drunk on both, he finally said, 'Yes.'

He did not wait till morning. That night, he went to the ford to renounce an old friendship. Although Cúchulainn pleaded with him, that two fosterlings of the Shadow Catcher should not battle, no words could sooth him now. They agreed to fight at first light.

As Cúchulainn walked away, a piece of holly pierced his foot, through skin and flesh to bone. He tore it out and threw it over his shoulder. The sharp shoot hit and passed through the nape of Fer Baeth's neck and he fell dead upon the ground. It has been known as Focherd in Muirtheimne – the Place of the Throw ever since.

Each night after that brought another warrior to Medb's tent and as the drink flowed another offer of her daughter's hand. But in the morning, no prospective bridegroom ever returned from his meeting with the warrior at the ford.

The king and queen sat together alone in their tent.

'If only we could get a great warrior like Lugaid mac Nois, the king of Munster, to face the Hound,' said Medb.

'He and Cúchulainn are old comrades,' said Ailill. 'And he is not someone to be so easily swayed by our daughter's affections.'

'What about his brother, Lairine, then?'

Ailill began to laugh. 'Lairine! He is strong, yes, but young and rough. Cúchulainn would make short work of him, to be sure.'

'Exactly,' said the queen. 'Then wouldn't Lugaid make short work of Cúchulainn to avenge his brother's death?'

Ailill smiled and looked at his wife as if to say, 'There really is no beating you!'

But tent walls are thin, and now Lugaid was already off to meet Cúchulainn at the ford.

'You are right welcome,' said the Hound.

'I trust that welcome,' said Lugaid. 'Indeed you should,' said Cúchulainn and the two warriors embraced.

'So you have not come to fight me then,' said Cúchulainn.

'No,' said Lugaid, 'but they intend to send my brother so that you might kill him and I would be forced to avenge his death. He is stupid and stubborn, but he is my brother and I ask when he comes, that you spare his life.'

'I will do my best,' said Cúchulainn, 'for the friendship that is between us.'

That night, Lairine was entertained royally in Medb and Ailill's tent, with Finnabair at his side.

'Don't they make a handsome couple,' said Medb.

'A future king and queen of Connacht,' said Ailill.

'If only we weren't being delayed by that pesky hound, then we could hold the wedding very soon.'

Lairine jumped up and the flock beds underneath him burst and through a storm of feathers, he cried, 'Tomorrow I will finish him and then we will make good what is promised here tonight.'

The next morning, Lairine brought a wagonload of weapons to the ford. Cúchulainn came unarmed. He took and broke the weapons as if depriving a little boy of his toy sword and shield. Then he squeezed Lairine between his hands and crushed him until all the shit flowed out of him and the waters stank and were made foul. Cúchulainn then cast him into the air and he landed alive outside his brother's tent. He was the only one to survive a battle with Cúchulainn at the ford, and yet he never lived as other men after that. He awoke with pain every morning, his stomach cramped when he ate, and his bowels no longer worked. Not a day went by without him wondering if it would have been better if he had been killed on that day at the ford.

A seasoned warrior by the name of Loch Mor mac Mo Febis was now shown to the tent. 'I will not fight a beardless boy,' he said. 'No matter how much your daughter smiles and winks.' So Medb sent her women to tell Cúchulainn to put a beard of blackberry juice upon his face. Seeing this, Loch agreed to fight him upstream, where the water had not been polluted by other men's shit and blood.

When they met there, the sky was turning dark.

The Crow Queen was descending, folding her tattered wings like a cloak around herself. She took the form of a white red-eared heifer charging. Cúchulainn flung his spear, pierced her thigh and brought her down.

She changed into a black and slippery eel and coiled herself around his legs. As he struggled to free himself, Loch slashed him across the chest. Cúchulainn roared with pain and then crushed the ribs of the black thing wrapped around his limbs.

She became a fierce wolf, snarling, but as she leapt, he cast a stone and took out one of her eyes. She screeched, became herself again, unfurled her wings and the storm was gone.

Loch was stabbing him in the arm. Then Laeg threw him the Gáe Bolga and he drove it into Loch's body. 'Step back from me,' said Loch. 'So that I may fall facing eastwards and not west towards the men of the four provinces, lest they think that I am retreating as a coward before you.'

'It is I who shall retreat,' said Cúchulainn, 'for it is only a true warrior who makes such a request.'

Cúchulainn yielded and Loch fell forward into the water.

Then came Cairbre Nia Fer, a King of Leinster, to meet him at the ford. Shield pressed against shield. The fighting was fierce and fast and both broke all their weapons. Then face-to-face with fists they fought, each pounding the other.

Now the fury was upon Cúchulainn, and he grasped Cairbre's head, twisted it off and raised it high into the air for all to see.

18

Massacre

Snow began to fall and the army of the four provinces settled on the plain of Murtheimne. As darkness came, a thousand campfires burned and flickered, making the warriors' shadows dance like giants across the land. Laeg watched as through tomorrow's battlefield, a figure came towards them.

'What do you see?' Cúchulainn asked.

'I see a golden sun rising.'

'Look again.'

'I see a swift deer leaping.'

'And what now?'

'I see a sharp spear flying.' Then a shining warrior stood between them.

'You have fought alone for long enough ma agrah, my son.'

Cúchulainn knew his father then. Laeg knelt, holding his spear before the Shining One.

'Rise, friend, Cúchulainn's loyal companion, always standing at his side, piercing that great loneliness.'

Then turning to his son, he said, 'Rest here awhile.'

Cúchulainn, who had been awake since the dying of the light at summer's end and had rested his head on the point of his spear each night so he would not sleep, now fell and his father caught him and held him in his arms and laid him down.

As his father began to sing to him there was another sound in the air.

Young voices calling, whistling, whooping as the boys from the north came to Cúchulainn's aid. As their fathers still rolled on the ground in the agony of labour, the young lads of Ulster had banded together to help their hero. When Ailill saw them coming, he sent out his fiercest men to face them and Laeg watched as the king's chariots raced out and surrounded the boys.

All the while as Cúchulainn slept his father murmured an enchantment over his body.

> 'Little hound stop your snapping at their heels,
>   Cease your howling at the moon.
> You are just a lad with the cuts and scrapes,
>   The marks of boyhood upon your body,
>   With my hands I bind you together again.'

Laeg watched and yelled as the spears flew and fell, tore and ripped through the boys on the frozen plain.

Lugh took herbs and chewed them and spat them into Cúchulainn's open wounds and taking his spear from the fire, he cauterised and stemmed the flow.

> 'Little hound of Culann, the smith,
>   who makes the sparks fly,
>   carried on the wind,
>   stars dance into the air,
>   dazzle our eyes
>   let fly a thousand spears.'

Now Laeg was watching just one lad still standing on the plain – Follamain, Conchobar's son, who was shouting, 'Come on big man, I will have your crown.'

Ailill sent out his two foster brothers and they soon cut him down.

> 'Little hound tears falling like snow,
>   soft across the plain,

a white blanket wraps its warmth
around you now.'

When Cúchulainn awoke, it was Laeg's face he saw.
'For how long have I slept?'
'Three days and nights.'
'Is Ulster overthrown?'
'No. The boys came and held them back.'
Cúchulainn stood up and looked across the plain and he could
see the frozen figures cloaked in the fallen snow.
'Yoke the scythe chariot.'
Laeg put on his tunic of skins, subtle and stitched, his mantle
of feathers, airy and light, his breastplate of iron, hard and heavy.
Then he brought the chariot with its iron points and sharp edges,
its hooks and its steel spikes, its nail-studded shafts, and the knives
that stuck out from the wheels.
Cúchulainn put on his twenty-seven tunics, waxed and
boardlike, bound with ropes against his soft skin to hold him
together when the distortions of battle came. Over those he put
on a battle girdle of hard leather, tough and tanned, made of
hide from seven ox yearlings. Then he took up his weapons, his
bright-faced sword, his five-pointed spear, his javelin, his eight-
razor rimmed shields and finally he put on his war helmet and
jumped into the chariot with Laeg beside him.
Within sight of the camp of the four provinces, Cúchulainn
saw the faces of the boys who had been slaughtered and then the
first distortion came upon him.
His shape began to shift. Each limb, each joint, began to move.
His sinews grew to the size of a warrior's fist as his feet and his
shins and his knees twisted to the back of his legs. One eye was
sucked into the red hollow of his head, while the other stuck out
as big as the head of a month-old child on his cheek. His hair
was on fire, the colour of red hawthorn used to cover the gap in
the boundary of a field. His cheeks peeled back from his jawbone
and his lungs and his liver fluttered in his throat. He howled as
if a god was trying to crawl his way out from beneath his skin.

As he circled the camp, everything inside him was in motion. At the first circuit, he performed the thunder feat of a hundred and a hundred men fell dead. At the second circuit he performed the thunder feat of two hundred and two hundred men fell dead. At the third circuit, he performed the thunder feat of three hundred and three hundred men fell dead, and on until he had performed six circuits of the camp and dead warriors lay six deep upon the ground. Of those that lived, it was said that not one man in three escaped without a broken thighbone, a split head, a smashed eye or without being marked for life in some way. Cúchulainn left without a scratch.

At dawn, a squinty-eyed old woman came limping, leading a cow with three teats. She began to milk. Cúchulainn asked her for a drink. She gave him milk from the first teat.

'The blessings of the gods and the non gods upon you,' said Cúchulainn and her leg was healed.

He asked for more and she gave him some milk from the second teat.

'The blessings of the gods and the non gods upon you,' said Cúchulainn and with that her eye opened again.

She gave him one more drink from the third teat.

'Great blessings of the gods and the non gods upon you,' said Cúchulainn and with that the Crow Queen was made whole again.

'Hah,' she cried. 'You said you would never heal me.'

'If I had known it was you, then I never would have.'

'But you did and that's what matters now. I came with a blessing, but you chose the curse. Things have almost run their course. Know that I'll have you in the end.'

19

Brothers
in Arms

There was only one man the queen now believed could beat the Hound face to face and that was his twin in nature and in skill, Ferdiad.

Medb sent messengers to him but he, knowing what she wanted, sent them back without a word. 'Not one word,' she said. 'Then I will send him many to cut through that hard hide of his.'

She dispatched three satirists and three lampoonists, knowing that words can wound deeper when wielded in different ways. They set about him with their armoury of acid accusations, riddles and epic revelations. Against these lacerating phrasemakers and sharp-witted shame singers he had little defence and as his honour was more important than his life, he finally journeyed back with them to the queen's camp. There she tried to seduce him with many gifts, the chief amongst them her daughter, Finnabair. She was beautiful and he was young, but he still said 'no'.

'Well,' said Medb. 'Perhaps what the satirists say is true – that you will not go against Cúchulainn because you love him in every possible way.'

The next day his horses were harnessed and at the ford he wished the Hound a welcome.

'Surely the welcome should be mine,' said Cúchulainn, 'for it is you that have come to meet me on my land.'

'You claim the world as yours,' said Ferdiad, 'and yet the world now wants its share.'

'We used to fight against the world, my dear brother,' said Cúchulainn, 'side by side in every battle and contest, in every wood and wasteland and then sleep a deep sleep in each other's arms, dreaming of the carnage we had caused.'

'Boys can sleep together. Men must fight together,' said Ferdiad. 'That is one lesson Scathach never taught. It is one I have learned from life.'

'It is not life that brings you here now,' said Cúchulainn, 'but death. If we fight, bonds will be broken, memories erased. All will be lost.'

'The only loss I seek here is yours,' said Ferdiad.

'The only loss you will find here is yours,' said Cúchulainn. 'Choose your weapons.'

'Battle darts,' said Ferdiad.

These flew like bees humming through the air from early morning to midday, back and forth and yet not one wound did they make.

'What weapons shall we use now, Cúchulainn?' asked Ferdiad.

'The choice is yours until nightfall,' replied the Hound.

'Then let us cast our smooth spears with their thongs of hard flax,' said Ferdiad.

When darkness came, each had been reddened and wounded by the other, and they went towards each other and put an arm around the other's neck and each kissed the other three times.

That night Cúchulainn sent healing herbs to his opponent's camp and received food and strong drink from his old friend in return.

The next morning, they met at the ford again. 'What weapons shall we use today?' asked Cúchulainn.

'That is your choice until nightfall,' said Ferdiad.

'Then I choose long spears,' said Cúchulainn.

From twilight to sunset, they raced towards each other in their chariots, knocking great pieces out of each other through which birds could have flown. Darkness brought the same embrace and kiss and exchange of aid.

The next morning when they met, Ferdiad looked dark-faced and dull-eyed. 'Dear foster brother, give up this fight for a daughter who is not given to you for life but for death,' said Cúchulainn.

'I come to you as my own man. Not at some woman's bidding,' said Ferdiad. 'Should I part from you now, my name would be held in high contempt. What weapons shall we use today?'

'The choice is yours,' said Cúchulainn, 'For I chose yesterday.'

'Let us take our heavy swords then,' said Ferdiad.

'Let us do so indeed,' said Cúchulainn.

All day long, they hacked and cut deeply into each other, until finally the night came again.

In the morning, Cúchulainn watched as Ferdiad practised many wonderful feats that he had not been taught by Scathach or any other but he had invented on that very day.

'Look at that,' said Cúchulainn to Laeg. 'Surprise is on his side now. If you see him getting the upper hand, I want you to shout out insults at me. But if I am winning, I want you to sing in praise of my valour.'

The two men met. 'What feat of arms shall we perform today?' asked Cúchulainn.

'It is your turn to choose,' said Ferdiad.

'Let us perform the feat of the ford,' said Cúchulainn.

'Let us do so indeed,' said Ferdiad.

All morning each cast all they had at the other and by midday they were fighting fiercer and closer together, so close that their faces met above, their feet met below and their hands met protected by shields in the middle, so close that they clove and split their shields from rim to centre, so close that their spears bent and turned and yielded to pressure from points and rivets, so close that they forced the river from its course and now fought on dry ground. Such was their closeness that the horses of Ireland went mad and broke their tethers and ran wild again. Such was their closeness that it was easy for Ferdiad to plunge a sharp blade into Cúchulainn's breast and as the blood dripped down his chest, the ford now flowed red.

Laeg shouted, 'He is the hawk and you are the mouse. He is the hound and you are the fox. He is the wolf and you are the rabbit. I have seen women fight fiercer than you. Braver boys! Call yourself a warrior? You are not even a man!' With these words came the first distortion on Cúchulainn. As he twisted and grew, Laeg threw him the Gáe Bolga; the weapon that made one wound when it entered a man's body, but thirty when it left it. Cúchulainn cast the weapon and it entered Ferdiad through his backside and inside pierced every organ with its barbs. No sooner had Ferdiad fallen, than Cúchulainn was holding him in his arms.

'We were whelps together once,' said Ferdiad, 'snapping at each other's heels. All was play and rough and tumble then, but now my brother brings about my end.' Then he breathed his last breath and Cúchulainn wept.

'Fair Ferdiad
There was nothing as dear to me
As your perfect form and face,
Your bright clear eyes your sweet speech
Which soothed in battle and in bed.
My match in fierceness, courage and in heart.

'The red-mouthed war goddess claims you now.
Many have I killed
Yet all was just play and sport
Until I met you,
My foster brother,
At the ford.

'Sad the fate that befalls us, the fosterlings of Scathach.
Yesterday you were as huge as a mountain
Today only your shadow remains.'

20

WOUNDS

The Ulstermen rose from their birth pangs and carried Cúchulainn's exhausted hulk into the waterways. They plunged him into the strong currents of the Sas, the steady stream of the Buan, the fresh waters of the Bithlan, the clear waters of the Findglais, the bright water of the Gleoir, the wild Glenamain, the gushing Bedg, the still Tadg, the silent Telameit, the deep Rind, the wide Bir, the bitter waters of the Bremide, the shallow waters of the Bichaem, the hidden stream of the Miliuc, the narrow flow of the Cumung, the trickle of the Gainemain, the Drong, the Delt and the black waters of the Dubglass.

Into each he was plunged, clear currents cleansing the cuts, cool waters washing away the blood from the wounds and the gashes until he was made whole again.

Now another man was on the move.

Naked and unarmed, Cethern mac Fintain, hurtled in his chariot towards the Ulster host. He flailed with fists and fingernails, inflicting wounds on everyone on every side and was assailed by point of spear and edge of sword and suddenly was fully exposed, his insides hanging out.

He rode on, holding himself together somehow, to the water's edge where Cúchulainn himself had just been healed.

'I see you are a man with guts!' Cúchulainn cried. Then, turning to his healers, said, 'fix this one too!'

The physicians hesitated, not wishing to help a warrior who they knew to be cantankerous even when he didn't have blood spurting out of him in all directions.

Cúchulainn warned them that they might soon be needing their skills for their own injuries if they did not tend his wounds and fast.

No further encouragement was needed.

The first physician came, examined him and said, 'This wound will kill you.'

'You too,' cried Cethern as he splattered the healer's brains across the ground. Another came and another. Each said the same. Fifty were dispatched in similar fashion.

'Have you no better than these?' Cethern asked.

'They came to help you,' said Cúchulainn.

'They just brought me bad news,' said Cethern.

'As you have to them,' said Cúchulainn surveying the corpses on the ground.

He sent for Fingein, the king's physician, to come and Cethern showed him each gash, stab and cut.

'This wound here,' said Fingein, 'is slight, made by one of your own kin, meaning no harm.'

'A young man with a crest of hair gave me that,' said Cethern, 'and I dealt him a slight one in return.'

'That man was Illand, the old king's son. He did not wish to hurt you and left a mark only so his comrades would not call him coward.'

'Examine this wound for me now,' said Cethern.

'This wound goes deeper,' said Fingein. 'It is made by a woman who always wants her own way.'

'A woman indeed,' said Cethern. 'Tall and pale, protected by breast plate of iron, a serrated spear blazing in her hand.'

'That woman was Medb, the queen, who wanted to add your head to her trophy cabinet.'

'Examine this one then,' said Cethern.

'This wound is black,' said Fingein, 'and made by two men whose spears entered your heart and crossed within it.'

'Yes! Two young fellows,' said Cethern. 'They came at me with their two spears and I defeated both with my one.'

'They were Bunn and Mecconn, two of the queen's warriors who prematurely boasted of your fall.'

'And these wounds, Master Fingein?'

'Those are many but not so deep,' said Fingein, 'and were made by two brothers.'

Cethern laughed, 'Yes they were alike in dimension and in deed. Each with a golden crown upon his head.'

'They were Broen and Brudne, the two sons of the three lights, who wanted to turn your world dark.'

'And this great wound here, my fine physician?'

'This wound is deadly,' said Fingein. 'It was made by a father and son working together.'

'I could see the likeness in the younger one's eyes,' said Cethern. 'That was Maine Condasgeib Uíle with his father the king, Ailill. And these three wounds here?'

'These wounds I cannot treat,' said Fingein. 'They were made by three mad men from the other world.'

'I could see the madness in the bastard's eyes,' said Cethern. 'They were the three nephews of Cú Roí mac Dàire, Carver, Divider and Server and they have severed the sinews of your heart. Now it rolls around your body like a bloody head in an empty bucket.'

'And this wound?'

'This wound was made in the morning.'

'And this?'

'This one was made under the stars by warriors too numerous to count.'

Each of the wounds was examined and its story recounted and in the telling some were healed, but not all.

'I am in your hands,' said Cethern. 'What does the future hold for me now?'

Fingein looked him in the eye and said, 'Let your cattle be butchered, for you will not be here to tend the calves in the spring.'

'The others who brought me such bad news, I butchered,' said Cethern.

'It was not their diagnosis that was wrong,' said Fingein. 'Just their bedside manner.'

'So I have no choice then.'

'There is always a choice,' said Fingein.

'Then what is mine?' asked Cethern.

'Leave the battlefield now,' said Fingein, 'and have time to say farewell to your kin and put your affairs in order, or I can fix you up and you can face your enemies one last time.'

'I choose the quicker death,' said Cethern.

'Make a marrow mash,' commanded Fingein.

Cúchulainn crushed together the flesh, the skulls, the hides of flocks and herds, and into this mash of blood and bone, Cethern was buried.

⁂

Someone else came, riding naked, everything on display. A forgotten god, his long, thin prick dangling dangerously between the chariot shafts, the wisdom of the world concealed within the wrinkles of his craggy sack. It was Illech, riding in his rickety old chariot, his own creaking frame defended by his rusty iron shield and his grandson's mighty sword. The chariot was full to the rim with rocks and stones and two broken-backed nags buckling beneath its weight. 'I come to fight the men of the four provinces,' he cried.

They laughed and jeered. 'First they send us their boys to fight. Now it is their old men they want us to slaughter.'

Their commander Dochae mac Magach shut them up. 'An old wolf can still bite.'

Then the stones rained down upon their heads and when his armoury of earth ended, some were injured, others left for dead.

'Respect your elders,' the old one cried and, seeing the marrow mash made of Ulster's beasts, he made another from the blood and bones of Connacht men, which he crushed between his arms and thighs.

Then, turning from the bloody mess to Dochae mac Magach, said, 'My time is passed. Take this sword and then my head and return both to their master.'

All was done as he had wished.

For three days and nights Cethern lay in the marrow mash, absorbing the goodness as the marrow entered the wounds and gashes, the cuts and hacks that covered his body. Ready, he rose, and pressing his belly against the board of the chariot to keep himself together, he took back the sword brought by his wife coming from the north.

Cethern commanded that his cattle and estates be divided equally between her and Fingein the great healer who had given him back his life, so that he could have an honourable death.

'I take the vengeance for my own death upon myself. I slay my own killers, so the descendants of those I kill will have no claim upon my kin.'

Now, there is no more frightening foe than one who has risen from the dead. King Ailill placed his crown and cloak upon a pillar stone, hoping that Cethern would mistake it for himself. In his fierce fury, Cethern drove his sword through the stone and then cried, 'Is there not a man of flesh and blood amongst you who is willing to face me?'

Maine Condasgeib Uile took his father's crown and cloak and advanced towards Cethern, who with the edge of his shield cut him into three. Then all the armies attacked Cethern from every side and he was brought down, but in truth, it was an old wound inflicted by a father and a son that got him in the end.

21

THE BULLS

A lone warrior rode into Emain Macha crying out, 'Our sons are slain, our women carried off, our cattle driven away.'

The Ulstermen were silent for it was forbidden for them to speak before their king and the king was silent, because it was forbidden for the king to speak before the seers.

The warrior kept on crying out, 'Our sons are slain, our women carried off, our cattle driven away,' repeating these words until his horse reared up and his own shield turned against him, the rim slicing off his head. The horse turned with the shield upon its back and the head upon the shield. And still the head cried out, 'Our sons are slain, our women carried off, our cattle driven away.'

Then the seers spoke. 'The sky is still above us, the earth is still beneath us, the sea still surrounds us. Unless the sky, with its showers of stars, falls, unless the earth erupts and spews fire, unless the sea rises from its bed and drowns us all, our sons will be called heroes, our women returned to sovereignty and our cattle brought back to their pasture. Men of Ulster arise.'

Mac Roth, Ailill's chief messenger, was the first to hear the great thunder coming. 'The stars have fallen from the skies. The earth has burst its surface. The sea has engulfed the land.'

He thought as he saw the creatures rushing out of the forest, covering the plain, so no piece of green could be seen.

'What does this mean?' asked Ailill.

'The thunder you hear is just the Ulstermen on the move,' said Fergus, 'The wild creatures flee before them.'

Then Mac Roth saw a grey mist coming. And in the mist, there were dark voids devouring the land where snow fell and birds flew. 'What does this mean?' asked Ailill.

'The mist you see is just the breath of the Ulstermen's horses fast approaching,' said Fergus. 'The voids – their mouths and nostrils flaring as they inhale and exhale the sun. The snow is the froth from their mouths, the birds, the clods of earth flung up by their hooves.'

Then Mac Roth saw a great firestorm coming, sparks flying, stars exploding, suns blazing.

'What does this mean?' asked Ailill.

'The fire you see is just the heat of the rage of the warriors of Ulster growing nearer,' said Fergus. 'The sparks of blazing fire are their fierce eyes filled with fury. The exploding stars the smiting of their spears, the blazing suns, the clashing of their swords on their shields.'

'They are just men like any other,' said Medb, turning on her heel off to rally her fighting men.

That night as the two armies watched each other across the plain, they heard the cry of the Crow Queen rising between them.

> 'Crows clawing and gnawing at necks.
> Flesh hacked and made fresh.
> Blades bloodied in battle.
> A forest of men cut down.
> Trunks severed, arms piled up in heaps,
> Red spurting and spilling on skin,
> Warriors warring and whoring
> My husbands, my sons, my lovers
> Come, dance with me again.'

A hundred men died of fright at the cry of the Crow Queen, and all through the night, Queen Medb chanted:

'Arise the tribes and triads of Ireland
the three Conalls from Collanair
the three Fiachras from Fidnemain
the three Lóegaires from Lecc Derg
the three Finns from Finnabair
the three Conirires from Sliab Mis
the three Lussens from Luachiair
the three Niad Chorb from Tialch Loiscthe
the three Damaltachs from Derdech
the three Bodars from Buas
the three Malleths from Loch Erne
the three Mac Amras from Ess Ruaid
the three Scathglaus from Scaire
the three Fintans from Fenen
the three Aedes from Aidne
the three Guaires from Gabal

'Then know the three smiles worse than sorrow
The smile of snow as it melts
The smile of your wife after she has been with another man.
The smile of a hound as it is ready to leap.'

The next morning, Fergus came carrying his wooden sword to the king and the queen. 'If only I had my own sword back,' he said, 'then I would pile the bodies, the limbs and the heads of the Ulstermen at your feet.'

'It lies safe beneath my pillow,' said Ailill, who commanded that it be brought and then the sword was given back into the old king's care.

He seized it and took it to the battlefield and found there the only man he wanted to kill – King Conchobar. Conchobar raised his shield, against Fergus's mighty blows. But he could not defend himself against the old king's words, 'Tyrant! Murderer of men! Betrayer of women! Usurper of Kingdoms! Feel the rage of one who once ruled all, who now cannot even hold the length of his own stride in his own land. Forced to dwell with deer and fox and hare under a queen whose sole subject is herself.'

Between the blows, Conchobar replied, 'All you say is true, and more. And yet I am still younger and mightier than you are. It takes a noble man to stomach the dirty work of kingship.'

With one last blow, Conchobar's shield was torn in two and Fergus would have taken off his head there and then, had not Conchobar's son, Cormac, rushed in between them both and said, 'Master Fergus! Do not cut off the blood that flows from our ancestors. Do not, great warrior of Ulster, kill the king of your people.'

Then Fergus swung his sword and took off the tops of three nearby hills instead.

Cúchulainn was now at his side, 'Foster father, flee now, as I once fled for you.'

Then Fergus, with three great strides, was back with Medb, who was now retreating fast. 'It is almost my time,' she said.

Fergus commanded her warriors to form a ring of shields to shelter her and as the moon rose, her waters flowed and three streams of blood snaked across the land.

Then the Donn Cuailnge, the great brown bull of Ulster, bellowed three times and the mighty Finnbennach, the white bull of Connacht, tossed his head as the two met on the plain.

The warriors chose Bricriu to judge the contest, for he was no fairer to his friends than he was to his enemies.

The two bulls stamped the ground and shook the earth. Their eyes blazed and their nostrils swelled like a smith's bellows at the forge. Then each charged and tore into the other, piercing the skin, tearing into the flesh, and Bricriu was trampled underneath and the bitterest tongue in Ulster was silent.

All day long they raged and fought. All night long the people of Ireland listened to their bellows and roars in the dark.

Then all was silent and everyone slept.

The next morning as a red sun rose, they saw the great brown bull coming from the west, carrying the mangled remains of the

Finnbennach on his horns. He tossed his head and raced through the land tearing up the earth, rooting out the forests, scattering the remains; the shoulder blade, loins, rib cage and liver across the whole of Ireland. Then exhausted, the mighty heart of that great beast burst and the quarrel between the two pig keepers was settled at last.

22

Dog Meat

Cúchulainn returned, worn out and weary from war. He had seen many foemen fall and as many friends, some by his own hand. Yet though his enemies were now dead, the sons of the slain were growing fast into men without the guidance of their fathers. Queen Medb gathered these orphans in and reared them as her fosterlings, weaning them on tales of the death and destruction.

'Erc, son of Cairbre Nia Fer, I saw your father's head held high, bloody for all the world to see.'

'Children of Cailitin, I saw your father and your brother's lives turned to stone at the ford.'

'Lugaid, son of Cú Roí mac Dáire, I saw your father tied to the bed post and your mother dashed on the rocks below.'

When they were all full of her words of blood and broken bones, these children went out into the world to avenge their fathers.

Cúchulainn heard their screams from across the plains. He called to Laeg to harness his horses and fetch his chariot. But the loyal charioteer returned alone and on foot.

'The Grey will not come,' he said. 'He has never refused me before, yet neither I nor my brothers could harness him today. Come and speak with him yourself.'

Cúchulainn went to the stables. 'Come to my hand, my Grey.'

But the horse turned away.

'Come to my hand.' A second time, the horse turned away.

Three times Cúchulainn called and three times the horse turned his back on his master, until Cúchulainn asked, 'Have I no friends left in this world?'

At these words, the Grey of Macha went between the shafts of the chariot, but as he went, they say he was weeping tears of blood.

Leborcham, the king's eyes and ears, and the ladies of Emain Macha cried, 'Cúchulainn! Go to the valley of silence. There, no scream will pierce the air.'

But Cúchulainn would not heed them. He rode instead, with Laeg beside him to his mother's house.

'I am thirsty,' he said, and Dectera brought him a cup full to the brim. But when he put it to his lips, he tasted blood. He dashed the cup upon the ground. She brought him another but he still saw red and crushed it into fragments.

'Have even you no comfort for me?' he asked.

The third cup tasted the same to him and he spat out the bitterness he found there.

'Stay here with me, my son,' she said. 'Your luck has deserted you and you are no longer safe in this world.' But he would not listen. Instead he kissed her and rode on until he came to the crossroads, where three old, one-eyed women sat around a fire. They were roasting meat on spits made from rowan.

'Ah!' said the first. 'You have come to give us poor midwives the pleasure of your company at last. What a whirlwind you are. Here. Eat with us. It's good roast dog.'

They offered him some meat, but he shook his head, 'I am forbidden to eat the flesh of a dog.'

The old women exchanged their one-eyed glances. The youngest shook her head, 'Look at you, all high and mighty now!'

The middle sister said, 'Too grand to take the food that a poor woman has to offer'.

'If this feast was offered to you by a king, you would surely eat it,' said the oldest one.

Poor, weak and old as they seemed, rather than offend them, he reached down and he took the shoulder blade of the hound in his left hand and bit into it. As he did, all the strength drained away from his left side.

He rode on to where the sons of the slain were waiting. Beside the lake, they had set up three pairs of warriors sparring and between each, there stood a satirist. 'Bring peace here!' the satirist cried.

'I will,' said Cúchulainn and he dashed out the brains of the first two warriors.

'Now give me your spear,' said the satirist.

'No,' said Cúchulainn. 'There is none that needs it more than me today.'

'Then I will sing of your meanness until my last breath, if you do not let me have it,' and he reached out his hand.

'Very well. You have it,' said Cúchulainn and he lifted his spear. The satirist, realising what he had said, turned to flee. Cúchulainn flung his spear; it passed through the head of the satirist, and now he had a metal tongue, which he could not wag.

'Who will fall by this spear?' asked the sons of the slain.

'A king will fall by this spear,' cried the children of Cailitin. They pulled it out of the head of the satirist and flung it back at Cúchulainn. Laeg leapt in front of the Hound, embraced him and, as he did, he took the full force of the blow. Cúchulainn held him close.

'Today you will have to be warrior and charioteer,' gasped Laeg.

'And tomorrow,' said Cúchulainn, 'I will be your charioteer in the other world,' and then the king of charioteers was no more.

Cúchulainn rode on to the second pair of warriors feigning a fight. 'Bring peace here!' cried the second satirist. 'Or else face the infamy of it!'

Cúchulainn tore the two warriors to pieces. 'Now give me the spear,' demanded the satirist.

'I have great need of it today,' said Cúchulainn.

'Then I will revile you,' cried the satirist.

'I have already paid for my honour today,' said Cúchulainn. 'I am not bound to defend it twice.'

'Then I will call the land on which you stand, rotten,' said the
satirist, 'and without worth if you do not let me have it.'

'Very well,' said Cúchulainn and he let loose his spear, piercing the head of the turning satirist so now he too was spitting
iron.

And Erc took the spear and pulled it out of the head of the
satirist. 'Who will fall by this spear?' he asked.

'A king will fall by this spear,' cried the sons of the slain.
And Erc flung it back at Cúchulainn. But as he did, the Grey
of Macha reared up and it pierced the horse's side. Cúchulainn
jumped down from the chariot, he pulled out the spear and
released the Grey from the chariot and, wounded, the Grey
raced away.

The king of horses was gone.

Cúchulainn drove on with only the black Sainglenn to pull his
chariot now, and he dealt swiftly with the third pair of warriors.

'Give me your spear,' cried the third satirist, 'or else I will
shame you.'

'I have already paid for my honour today,' said Cúchulainn.

'Then I will revile your land,' said the satirist.

'I have already paid for Ulster's honour today,' said Cúchulainn.

'Then I will revile your race,' said the satirist.

'Have it then,' said Cúchulainn and the last satirist fell silent.

Lugaid, the son of Cú Roí mac Dáire, took the spear and
asked, 'Who will fall by this spear?'

'A king will fall by this spear,' cried the sons of the slain. And
Lugaid flung it and it struck Cúchulainn in the chest. The yoke
of the chariot broke then and the king of warriors fell to the
ground. He clutched at the wound and holding himself together,
he spoke to the sons of the slain.

'Give me leave to go to the lake to quench my thirst.' They
granted it.

When Cúchulainn returned, he tied himself to a standing
stone so that he would not die like a dog on the ground.

Then the sons of Cairbre said, 'Let us take his head as he took
our father's.'